Haila Troy. A former model, now an actress, with a nose for trouble.

Jeff Troy. A photographer and wisecracking amateur detective.

Austin Marshall. Commodore of the Knickerbocker Model Yachting Club. He's a man of many hobbies.

Bernard Marshall. Austin's indolent younger brother and a fellow member of the Knickerbockers.

Carl Marshall. Austin's nephew, a young soldier on leave.

George Mead. A fierce old man in a wheelchair and a charter member of the Knickerbockers.

Penny Mead. His pretty daughter, whom Carl badly wants to marry.

Tony Gilbert. A handsome, sarcastic actor, also a Knickerbocker.

William Phillips. A gaunt, sour-faced, and wealthy Knickerbocker.

Diane Phillips. His sultry, much younger wife.

Marjorie Davisson. She's having a flirtation with Tony Gilbert.

Walter Davisson. Her husband, a radio psychologist known to millions as The Marriage Doctor.

Robert Nichols. A music teacher whose daughter has gone missing.

Harley Olsen and Lettie. A happy couple in Hoboken.

Mrs. Clancy. The Troys' cleaning woman. She and her seven-year-old son **Chuckie** got the Troys into this mess.

Lieutenant Detective Hankins. A homicide detective.

Bolling. His assistant. He's full of theories about what happened.

Books by Kelley Roos

Featuring Jeff & Haila Troy

Made Up To Kill (1940)*
If the Shroud Fits (1941)*
The Frightened Stiff (1942)*
Sailor, Take Warning! (1944)*
There Was a Crooked Man (1945)
Ghost of a Chance (1947)
Murder in Any Language (1948)
Triple Threat (1949)
One False Move (1966)

* reprinted by Rue Morgue Press
as of August 2006

Other mystery novels

The Blonde Died Laughing (1956)
Requiem for a Blonde (1958)
Scent of Mystery (1959)
Grave Danger (1965)
Necessary Evil (1965)
A Few Days in Madrid (1965
(Above published as by Audrey and William Roos)
Cry in the Night (1966)
Who Saw Maggie Brown? (1967)
To Save His Life (1968)
Suddenly One Night (1970)
What Did Hattie See? (1970)
Bad Trip (1971)
Murder on Martha's Vineyard (1981)

Sailor, Take Warning!

A Jeff & Haila Troy mystery by
Kelley Roos

Rue Morgue Press
Lyons / Boulder

The Rue Morgue Press
P.O. Box 4119
Boulder, Colorado 80306
800-699-6214
www.ruemorguepress.com

Printed by
Johnson Printing

PRINTED IN THE UNITED STATES OF AMERICA

Meet the Authors

Kelley Roos was the pseudonym used by the husband-and-wife writing team of William and Audrey Kelley Roos who, like their contemporaries, Frances and Richard Lockridge, wrote about a husband-and-wife detective team. Photographer (though he tried his hand at other careers) Jeff Troy and his future wife, actress Haila Rogers, were introduced to the reading public in 1940's *Made Up To Kill*, the same year that saw the birth of the Norths. They received a five hundred dollar advance for their first effort and never looked back.

Eight more adventures featuring the Troys appeared before they abandoned the series in 1966 (there had been a 17-year vacation from the series between book eight and book nine). The books, laced with wisecracks and filled with screwball humor, have the feel of a 1940s movie comedy. In fact, the third Troy mystery, *The Frightened Stiff*, was filmed in 1943 as *A Night to Remember* with Loretta Young and Brian Aherne playing the Troys. They wrote numerous non-Troy mysteries as well and received an Edgar for the 1960 television play, *The Case of the Burning Court*, based on the novel by John Dickson Carr.

William Roos was born in Pittsburgh, Pennsylvania, in 1911, and he was graduated from Carnegie Tech in Pittsburg where he was enrolled in the drama department with an eye toward becoming a playwright. It was there that he met Audrey, who was studying to be an actress. Born in Elizabethtown, New Jersey, in 1912, she had been raised in Uniontown, Pennsylvania. After graduation, Audrey took a touch-typing course (William never learned) and the two headed for New York City. Audrey eventually gave up her dream of becoming an actress and decided to write a detective novel. William soon became attracted to the idea as well and initially the two would plot their books over drinks in the evening. At first they wrote alternate chapters and then passed them on to each other for rewrites. Eventually, William wrote the entire first drafts but, with William still unable to touch-type, Audrey always had the last word.

They lived in Connecticut and Spain as well before finally settling in the late 1960s in an old whaling captain's house on Martha's Vineyard, where Audrey died in 1982 and William in 1987. For more information on their lives and collaborations, see Tom and Enid Schantzes' introduction to The Rue Morgue Press edition of *The Frightened Stiff.*

Sailor, Take Warning!

CHAPTER ONE

THE subway train slowed for the Seventy-seventh Street station and I nudged Jeff. He opened one eye and fixed me with a malevolent glare. He put a curse on me that extended through the fiscal year of 1999. He made an eternal reservation for me in the hot place. Jeff was behaving very badly.

And I had been so proud of him.

Mrs. Clancy, our cleaning woman … two hours per afternoon, fifty cents per hour … had been invited to a wedding. But there was her small son, Chuckie. If she took him to the wedding, she wouldn't catch even a glimpse of the bride, since Chuckie needed not one eye kept on him, but two. He wasn't really wicked, Mrs. Clancy said, just too full of Vitamin B.

Magnanimously, Jeff had solved her problem. We would, this Sunday afternoon, take Chuckie to the park. We would love doing it. Central Park was at its best in September; September was at its best in Central Park. His lyricism almost made me buy a new dress and a matching parasol for the outing.

Going up the subway steps to Lexington Avenue, Jeff said, in a voice of doom doubled, "Where is this little hellion kept?"

"Seventy-fifth. East of here."

"Haila, I just remembered! I've got to get to the studio right away! There's a camera that I should ..."

"Oh, no, you don't!" I grabbed his arm. "After all, this was your idea."

"It was my idea for *you* to take Chuckie."

"Hurry, darling, Mrs. Clancy will miss 'Oh, Promise Me.' "

Upon the steps of the address on my mental note sat a small boy, aged approximately seven. There was a toy boat in his lap. There was a definite Clancy cast to his button nose.

I said, "Are you Chuckie?"

"I am Chuck," the boy said. "Are you Mrs. Troy?"

"Yes. Where's your mother?"

"Where do you think, you're late, she went. I promised to sit here until you came, that's your husband, huh?" Chuckie inspected Jeff from head to foot. "He's big, isn't he?"

"Yeah," Jeff said. "So don't start anything."

"If you wanna fight," Chuckie yelped, "join the Army!"

"He has," I said, hoping to promote a little good will. "He's waiting to be called. Into the Air Force."

Chuckie leaped to his feet. "Will you take me up in your plane?"

"I'll take you up," Jeff said, "but I won't bring you down."

"I'll use my parachute!" He flung himself off the top step and landed on the sidewalk, bottom down. The sidewalk winced, but not our paratrooper. He bounced back on his feet.

"C'mon! Uncle Austin will be gone!"

Jeff said, "You have an uncle and we've got to take care of you?"

"He isn't really my uncle. Uncle George and Uncle Bernie and Uncle Tony, they aren't really my uncles, neither."

"You've got a lot of people who aren't your uncles."

"Can I call you Uncle Jeff?"

"You cannot. Where are these uncles?"

"In the park sailing their ships, where do you think?"

"Sailing their ... how old are they?" Jeff asked.

"Some of them are about a hundred, some of them aren't. I bet the hundred ones even could lick you."

"Not one-handed, I bet. Let's go, I want to see these ancient mariners. Shall I carry your boat?"

"No, you might break it." Chuckie glanced at me. "Do we have to take her along?"

"What's wrong with me?" I demanded.

He smiled pityingly and turned to Jeff. "What did you have to marry a girl for? Beat you to the corner!"

Chuckie beat us to that corner and every corner all the way to Fifth Avenue. There Jeff surprised me by dragging him from the path of a large, revolving wheel attached to a large, heavy bus. Without a word of thanks, our charge scooted across to the park side of the street, scrambled over the stone wall and disappeared. We pursued him hotly.

Jeff vaulted the wall; I stepped up on a bench and clambered over it sidesaddle. No Tarzan's Mate, I.

"Where's Chuckie?" I asked. "At the bottom of the lake?"

"Not yet," Jeff said, and started running.

I saw Chuckie then, rushing headlong down the slope toward the water's edge. Only a miracle … or hydraulic brakes … could save him from a public bath. The miracle happened. A man, crouched over the rim of the lake, rose, turned and caught the child in his arms. He lifted him high in the air in that adult welcome of the very young. Jeff and I slowed to a walk.

Chuckie's friend was a man in his late forties, tall and thickly set. From beneath a yachting cap a forelock of black hair fell boyishly across his brow. Over a white jersey he wore a blue coat of a definitely seafaring cut. His trousers had certainly been washed up on some beach, although one of the better beaches. But the picturesqueness of this man was completely uncontrived. He seemed as unselfconscious as Chuckie.

Jeff and I threaded our way through the nurses and their prodigies, the sun-seekers, the outdoor readers and the people who simply liked to sit and look at a little lake on which little boats bobbed merrily. A park attendant with a candy and ice cream store on wheels sent the children begging to their parents. Another khaki-clad employee with a pickup stick busily rid the area of fallen papers. There was something fabulous about the scene, something operetta-like, and only the silhouette of the towering apartments and hotels fifteen blocks south on Fifty-ninth Street kept you from forgetting that this was New York.

Chuckie started shouting at us at twenty paces. "Here's Uncle Austin!" he cried. "He's the Commodore!"

Uncle Austin turned to greet us, smiling. "I'm merely the Commodore of the Knickerbocker Model Yachting Club," he said, "which sails the sea before you on Saturday, Sunday and holiday afternoons. How do you do? My name is Marshall."

Jeff introduced us and we all shook hands, including Chuckie who, it turned out, considered handshaking very important. Austin Marshall laughed at him and patted his head. "Chuckie's our cabin boy," he said affectionately.

"You bet!" Chuckie shouted. "Uncle Austin, have you finished my Viking ship yet?"

"Almost, son."

"Uncle Austin's making me a Viking ship! The kind that discovered America before Christopher Columbus, Christopher Columbus didn't discover America until 1492 the sissy!"

"Do you make all your own models, Mr. Marshall?" I asked.

"Of course!" His heavy eyebrows leaped with surprise that I could imagine anything else. He stepped aside and pointed to the water below. "That's my latest masterpiece there. Like it?"

The Commodore had reason to be proud; his model ship actually was a work of art. But it didn't belong on a library mantel, nor in a bottle. It belonged in the water. Proud and graceful, it moved before us, convincingly realistic in its most minute detail. I counted three masts, so I said intelligently, "A three-masted schooner!"

Marshall merely smiled; Chuckie howled in disgust.

"No! It's a frigate, it's the Constitution! On August 19th, 1812, she ..."

"Careful, Chuckie," Jeff said solemnly. "No names, no dates, no places. There might be a Nazi agent around."

"Yes," Marshall said. "He'll radio what you say to a submarine captain and the Constitution will be torpedoed before she gets past Sandy Hook."

"Nazi spies," Chuckie said in a matter-of-fact tone, "shouldn't be allowed in Central Park. Hey, Mrs. Troy, there's a schooner!" He pointed excitedly to a model moving briskly across the lake with all sails set. "That's a Smuggler, Mrs. Troy!"

"Yes," Marshall said. "The Gloucester fishermen first built them around the eighteen-seventies. And because they were so fast the smugglers started using them."

"That's Uncle Tony's ship," Chuckie said.

A sudden gust of wind, probably a nor'easter, caught the Smuggler and sent it racing toward the concrete side of the lake. It was headed for a certain crash. Then a tall young woman in bright tweeds, her soft brown hair blowing in the quick wind, moved to the danger point. She crouched down, her arms outstretched to intercept the ship. But Austin Marshall evidently didn't trust women around the precious toys. With startling suddenness he rushed to her side, plunged down on all fours, and scooped the Smuggler out of the water before it touched her waiting hands. Then, cradling it protectively, almost lovingly, in his arms, he traded a few pleasantries with the girl and started back to us.

"Uncle Tony!" Chuckie yelped to a young man who was striding toward the Commodore. "Boy, that was a narrow one!"

Uncle Tony cut a dashing, a debonair figure. His model yachting outfit would have looked all right at Newport or in a Hollywood picture, as would Uncle Tony himself. He had all the requirements: the dark, curly hair, the straight, perfect profile, the height, the wide shoulders. In his hand he sported a malacca walking stick, which was just the right note to complete the celluloid version of the male romantic.

Now he was taking his ship from Marshall's hands with feverish eagerness, like a mother recovering her lost child. These model builders, it appeared, were fond of their handiwork. The Commodore steered him to us and introduced us.

His name was Tony Gilbert, his profession, unsurprisingly, acting. He lost no time at all in casually informing us that he was currently appearing in the Broadway smash hit, "Skirmish," at the Colony Theatre.

"Have you seen it?" he asked me.

"Not yet."

"Uncle Tony is the best actor in the world," Chuckie announced. "Aren't you, Uncle Tony?"

Gilbert laughed at the boy and said, "Well now, there's a guy named Muni who ..."

"Aaah, I bet he's older than you are!"

"That's it, Chuckie, and he gets the big parts. I get the small ones." He looked hurriedly at his watch. "One-thirty!"

"And you have a Sunday matinee," Jeff said.

"Right. Good-bye, drop backstage sometime. I give my best performances in my dressing room, my friends say. The lice!"

We watched the actor stride away. The Commodore smiled thoughtfully. "A nice chap," he said. "Come along, I want you to meet the rest of our club. It's rather depleted now, though, by the demands of war. Ironically enough, our Vice-Commodore is in Washington doing something about railroads."

Still chuckling over the Vice-Commodore's shame, Marshall led us through some more introductions. We met a William Phillips, a tall, gaunt, sour-faced gentleman, who smiled only when his eye fell on the huge Barkentine that he was sailing this sunny afternoon. We met the Commodore's brother, Bernard Marshall, a roly-poly man with a jolly face and a silent tongue, until the talk turned nautical, which it immediately did.

Leaving Chuckie in the care of these two old tars, we followed the Commodore away from that air now blued with binnacles, toggles, stanchions, struts, dead eyes, gaff jaws, winches and withes, and walked toward a man in a wheelchair. Beside him stood a girl. Our approach broke up a mounting quarrel between them. The girl's face did a quick change from exasperation to smiling welcome, but the man only shifted his angry glare from her to us.

He hated his wheelchair; you could see that at once. His strong, husky shoulders, his restless hands, his great, white-thatched head all seemed to be trying to leap from it. His eyes had the irate truculence of the unreconciled invalid. The girl, no more than twenty, was lovely with a fresh and natural prettiness. Her ash blonde hair was an invitation to the sunshine to do its dancing there, and it accepted. She stood very erect, as though to deny her five-foot-twoness.

Austin Marshall clapped the invalid affectionately on his back as he introduced us. "George Mead," he said, "one of our charter members. And his daughter Penny."

Penny smiled and nodded, but her father leaned forward abruptly in his chair. "Jeff Troy, eh? I know about you! Now, wait, don't tell me what you do … let me think."

Jeff bloomed with pride while the elderly man thought. "Maybe," he suggested, "you've seen some of the pictures I've taken."

"Nope! Didn't know you were a photographer."

Jeff's bloom faded, and brightened again. "In 1932 at Dartmouth I came in fifth against Cornell in the pole vault."

"Nope!"

Jeff was crestfallen. "That's all I've ever done, I'm afraid. You must be thinking of someone else."

"I've got it!" George Mead shouted. "You're the young fellow who solved those murders! Brilliant work, boy, brilliant! Especially that business down on Gay Street."

"Oh, yes," Penny said. "I remember that. Every half hour I had to go out for more newspapers. Father's an armchair detective, you see."

"Penny," her father said, cocking a scowling eyebrow at her, "I've got a good mind to hire Troy to keep an eye on you."

"Father, don't be silly!" The girl flushed, half in anger, half in embarrassment. She moved to the back of his chair and grasped its handle firmly. "It's time for your sun-nap now."

"Child!" roared Mr. Mead. "If you move this hellish contraption one inch from this spot, I'll have you boiled in oil!"

Penny ignored him. Nodding a good by at us, she set her jaw and hastily wheeled her protesting parent away. Austin Marshall grinned at their retreating figures, remarking what a fine old gentleman was Mead and what a fine girl his daughter. Then, shaking our hands, he said what a fine young couple we were, and returned to his ship at the lakeside.

Chuckie, by this time, had deserted William Phillips and Bernard Marshall and taken up with a sailor more his own age with whom he was playing happily. Jeff and I sat down on a bench at one end of the lake to wait out the time until Chuckie's homegoing.

The children had succeeded in wresting control of the water from the adult yachters and were making the most of it. A church bell on the Avenue behind us struck two and their shouting nearly drowned out its sonorous pealing. There was a great deal more screaming and splashing going on than seamanship. I was musing over how many children must fall in the lake per day when Jeff nudged me.

"The Commodore," he said, "could use a crew."

"What?"

"Look."

Austin Marshall was toting his good ship Constitution in a large, unwieldy case. He had left the lake and was climbing up the staired concrete walk that scaled one of those rocky promontories which dot Central Park. At the top was a single bench. Carefully placing his case upon it, he sat beside the case. Sunlight flashed off the lens of his spectacles as he slipped them onto his nose. He sat there, a motionless figure high above the clamor and color of the lakeside. A bare-legged ragamuffin ran screaming up the hill, hotly pursued by a villainous character of about nine armed to the teeth with a water pistol. They circled Austin and came tumbling down. A park attendant tidied up the knoll, spearing unsightly papers and depositing them in his bag. A fat woman lumbered halfway to the top, snapped a picture of the lake scene and puffed back down.

We sat there watching while the minutes drifted lazily by. Then Chuckie suddenly popped up at my side. "Mrs. Troy," he squeaked, "I want to ask Uncle Austin something about my ship! Can I go up and ask him can I?"

"Of course, but don't stay too long. It's two-twenty and we'll have to leave soon."

"I won't be long ... aw, heck! Mr. Phillips is going up to see Uncle Austin. I don't like Mr. Phillips ... heck!"

William Phillips was slowly climbing the Commodore's hill, approaching his bench. I watched him as he stood, tall and thin before Marshall, nodding his head in hearty agreement at something the other man had said. They chatted for a moment longer, then Phillips came down and headed for the Seventy-second Street park crossing.

I opened my mouth to tell Chuckie that now was his chance to see the Commodore, but he had already returned to his younger friend. I leaned back and let the sunlight pour over me, filling me with a wonderful inertia. From the lake Bernard Marshall, preparing to leave, waved good-bye to me. It was a physical effort for me to return his wave. Jeff's eyes were closed; he was dozing. He might as well have stayed at home for all the company he was. Every two minutes his head nearly rolled off his shoulders and each time he awoke grumbling from the shock. Finally he gave up and got to his feet.

He said, "I bet Chuckie would like an ice cream cone."

"I bet you would, too."

"Now that you mention it."

Jeff ambled away to the ice cream kiosk. I looked for Chuckie and spotted him racing around from the Fifth Avenue side of the lake. He had seen that his Uncle Austin was now unoccupied and was making a beeline for him. He zipped past me and up the rocky terrace. Almost immediately he was back again. His shanty Irish face was covered with woe.

"Uncle Austin," he said dismally, "won't speak to me."

"I'll speak to you. And in a minute Jeff ..."

"Uncle Austin always talks to me he likes me. But now he won't do anything but sit there and kind of smile with his mouth kind of open and ..."

I raised my head to look up at Austin Marshall. His gleaming spectacles beamed down with benevolence at the marine scene below him. But his hands rested in a stiffly awkward position in his lap and his shoulders were thrust back unnaturally, rigidly.

I stood up abruptly. "Chuckie, you wait here."

I started up the hill, the sound of my footsteps on the pavement growing increasingly louder in my ears as I neared the silent Commodore. I heard the noise of Chuckie's feet, kicking and scraping, as he chased behind me. I put out my hand and stopped him.

I had come close enough. Close enough to see that it had been only the sunshine bouncing off his glasses that made me think

Austin Marshall had been enjoying the lake view. And I was close enough to see the ugly little weapon, a thin, nail-like piece of steel, protruding from the back of his neck.

Hoping that my hands were steady, I put them on Chuckie's shoulders and turned him firmly around. For in another moment, he, too, might have seen that his Uncle Austin had been murdered.

CHAPTER TWO

I WAS in a taxi headed for home.

Jeff had swept us swiftly away from that death-tipped knoll. He had hailed a cab and given the driver two addresses, Chuckie's and 39 Gay Street, then he had disappeared into the park. Luckily, Mrs. Clancy had returned from the wedding and she had stepped wonderfully between her son and "Uncle Austin's sick." By the time I left she had succeeded in blotting from the boy's mind the sight he had seen.

I lit a cigarette and blew a cloud of smoke up before my eyes. But I could still see the back of the taxi driver's neck, still imagine that I saw a murderous sliver of metal sticking from it.

Then I was home on Gay Street, standing by our fireplace and watching our old studio couch turn into a Central Park bench. A bench on which Austin Marshall sat in the warming sun, thinking, perhaps, of a ship's model he was building for a boy named Chuckie. Not thinking, certainly, of a weapon that had been built for him.

I brewed a cup of tea and didn't drink it. I poured some brandy in a glass and returned it to the bottle. Twice I put on my hat to start for Central Park; twice I took it off. Jeff's parting instructions had been for me to wait here.

At last his knock bounced off our door, the ratatat-tat that meant someone was with him. Someone, indeed: Lieutenant Detective Hankins of the Homicide Bureau and his assistant, Bolling. They smiled in my direction; they remembered me. They glanced around the apartment and stopped smiling.

They remembered it, too, and a corpse in its garden.

"Mrs. Troy," Hankins said sadly, "we meet again."

"How are you, Mrs. Troy?" Bolling asked.

"Can the small talk," Hankins said, his eyes perfectly blank in his square, heavy face. You couldn't ever tell what Hankins was thinking, or if he was. But there was no doubt about Bolling. His earnest red face was continually wrinkled in the throes of mental desperation.

"Be seated," I invited. "Have a drink?"

"Yes," said Bolling.

"No," said Hankins.

"Thanks anyway," Bolling sighed.

"Mrs. Troy," said Hankins, "this afternoon you were sitting where you could see the victim clearly?"

"Yes."

"You saw him and a gent named William Phillips talking together?"

"Yes."

"How long after that did you discover that Marshall was dead?"

"Not more than ten minutes."

"In those ten minutes did you see anybody go near Marshall?"

"No, but it's possible that ..."

Hankins stepped closer to me, his voice a low growl. "From where you were sitting you would more than likely have seen anyone go up that hill?"

"More than likely," I said. "If it weren't a question of murder, I'd be positive."

"Sure," Hankins said mournfully. "And I got seven other witnesses who say nobody went up that hill. There's no doubt that no one went within fifty feet of the victim between the time he talked to Phillips and his death. The crime couldn't have happened, that's all. Why do I always get these impossible cases?"

"Nothing that happens is impossible," Bolling said.

Hankins turned a baleful eye on him. "And I got a philosopher for an assistant."

"Listen, Hank, I still maintain that nail-thing must have been fired into Marshall's neck. From a distance."

"Fired from what? A pea shooter? A rubber band? Or maybe some diabolical Oriental contrivance?"

"Well, maybe ..."

"No, Bolling," Hankins sighed. "This was a precision job, practically surgical. It was done by hand, by a strong, steady hand."

"It could have been projected from a distance," Bolling insisted. "In fact, it couldn't have happened any other way. Nobody went close enough to him to do it by hand."

"Maybe it didn't happen," Hankins said with weary sarcasm. "Maybe it's all a dream. Troy, what do you think?"

Jeff swung himself into a prone position on the studio couch, his hands behind his head. He smiled. "I agree with you, Hank. It couldn't have happened."

"A lot of help you are, Troy."

"I'm not helping at all. I like to solve cases and since this case is not going to be solved, it's all yours."

"Thanks." Hankins' laugh was grim. "The perfect crime, huh?"

"Well, too perfect for me."

Hankins eyed Jeff with suspicion. "Troy being modest, something's screwy. Do you know something I don't?"

"Yeah. I know when I'm licked."

"Stop it, Troy," Hankins said sourly. "You're giving me an inferiority complex."

"The both of you," Bolling said, "are being unduly pessimistic. This murderer is human; we're human. We'll get him. Cheer up, Hank."

"Aaah, shut up and stop smiling! And furthermore, this murderer isn't human! Is it human to be invisible? Don't answer me, Bolling, please! And that piece of steel was not fired from a distance!"

The phone rang in the next room and Jeff said, "I'll get it." Hankins watched him walk away, then he pulled his black fedora even further down on his head. "Mrs. Troy, it's been very unpleasant seeing you again. But I assure you, it's the circumstances. Unofficially, you're a nice girl. Well meaning."

"Cute, too," Bolling added. "Not actually beautiful, but very cute."

"You don't know anything." Hankins pushed his assistant out of the apartment. "She's beautiful."

That turned my head, so completely that I saw Jeff come back into the living room. "It was nobody," he grumbled. "At least nobody who wanted to talk to me. I say hello, they hang up."

"Jeff, I'm nice, well meaning, cute and beautiful!"

"No. You're nothing but a pair of knees. Saucy knees. That's all. How about some dinner?"

"I've got good knees? Wait till I look at them."

"I'll look at them. Hey, Haila!"

"Yes, darling?"

"The phone rings. I answer it. When the caller hears my voice, he hangs up. Well, what am I to think? Me being a jealous husband."

"The day you get jealous is the day I have my wedding ring cut to fit me. Jeff, who did you buy this ring for anyway? Certainly not for me!"

"Haila, don't start that again. On second thought, do. It'll keep your mind off murder."

"Oh, I've lost interest in that. I know who did it. If Hankins doesn't find out in a few days, I'll tell him."

Jeff laughed. "You think Phillips must have done it while he was talking to Marshall, don't you?"

"Yes! Well, he might have, mightn't he?"

"Be honest."

"All right, if you insist," I said irritably. "Unfortunately, I watched Phillips and Marshall while they were together. And Phillips was just talking to him, not pushing a sliver of steel into the back of his neck. Jeff, were any of the other members of the Yacht Club around afterwards?"

"No. But before the police arrived, Austin Marshall's young nephew popped up. He's a soldier, first lieutenant. On leave. A nice guy."

"He just happened to … pop up? Like that?"

"Sure. He was walking in the park, saw the crowd and investigated. He's spending his leave with Austin and his brother … their house is just across Fifth Avenue from the park. Why couldn't he just be walking in the …" Jeff stopped, came to me and put his hands unlovingly around my neck. "Listen, sweet," he said, "stop trying to get me interested in this case. It's not for Troy."

"Jeff, you underestimate yourself."

"Haila, you underestimate the murderer."

"He's human. Bolling said so."

"There's no place in this case to take off from, Haila. It happened in a vacuum. Speaking of vacuums, let's go out for dinner, shall we?"

It was fifteen minutes later, after we had scrubbed the dust of Central Park from ourselves, that I saw the long white envelope sticking out from beneath our hall door. I picked it up. On its face in rough block letters was printed: MR. JEFF TROY. PERSONAL. I took it to him.

Jeff split open the envelope and pulled out its contents. He whistled; I gasped. It wasn't every day that my husband held one thousand dollars in one hundred dollar bills in his hands. Gingerly, as if they were hot, he placed them on the coffee table. He read the note to me.

"Enclosed find part payment for solving the murder of Austin Marshall."

That was all. There was no signature. The writing was the same unrevealing block print as the writing on the envelope. Jeff's employer wished to remain anonymous.

We stood there looking at each other. Then we looked at the money. "Darling," I said, "we're rich!"

"Who sent it?" Jeff asked.

"Who cares?" I said.

"That phone call … it was to make sure I was at home."

"I'm going to buy myself a mink! And, Jeff, you can get a haircut! We're wealthy!"

He picked up the bills, stuffed them and the note into his breast pocket. He smiled at me. "Haila," he said briskly, "let's be on our way."

"Of course, Mr. Rockefeller, of course! What's our first stop?"

"George Mead."

"Why him especially?"

"Because he has a daughter named Penny."

"That kneeless little biddy? Jeff, since we're one of the Sixty Families now, let's take a Fifth Avenue bus. What's ten cents!"

"Put on your hat, Haila, if it still fits, while I phone Mead and make a date."

George Mead lived high in an apartment house that overlooked Fifth Avenue and Central Park. His butler defied tradition by greeting us warmly and genially ushering us into what was apparently the meeting place of the Knickerbocker Model Yacht Club. It was a large room, paneled in knotty pine, with windows cut in the shape of portholes, with nautically inclined furniture upholstered in awning-striped ticking. There were gleaming white life preservers and ship's lanterns and enough ship models to tell an almost unabridged history of the sea. As we entered a ship's clock merrily belled out the time, but not to this landlubber.

Our host wheeled his chair across the room at an alarming rate of speed, miraculously stopping just short of running us down. "I'm glad to see you!" he shouted. "You know everybody here, don't you?"

We knew Penny, who was curled up on a settee, looking at ease until you saw her clenched fists. And there was William Phillips, fidgeting morosely on the edge of a bench. We didn't know the woman who lay languorously in a deck chair. She swung her long, well-shaped legs to the floor with loving care. The lady had something there and she knew it. She rose and stepped toward us, a lazy half-smile of welcome on her face. She was about thirty-five, at the peak of her dark, disturbing beauty.

"I'm Diane Phillips," she said, then added, "William's wife." The words "not his daughter" were left unsaid, but they filled the room. She must have sensed that she had overmade her point, for she said hurriedly, "George, suppose we all have a drink, shall we?"

"Haila and I can only stay a moment," Jeff said. "You see, somebody … anonymously … sent me a thousand dollars to solve this case. I'd like to know who that person is."

Jeff looked questioningly at each person in the room. They looked questioningly at each other. If Jeff's employer was present, he wasn't admitting it. George Mead snapped the growing silence.

"Troy," he roared, "whoever hired you was smart! I wish I'd thought of it! Come on, boy, to work! Tear us to pieces! Find out which one of us murdered Austin!"

"See here, George!" Phillips said, the pompous authority of his voice belying his thin, almost spinsterish appearance. "Are you inferring that Austin was murdered by a member of the Yacht Club?"

"Why not? We knew his habit of sitting on that knoll for an hour or so every day! We knew where he'd be. Therefore, one of us could have planned this crime. We ..."

"Just a second!" Phillips was bristling. "Do you realize, George, what you're saying? You're saying that it was either I or Tony Gilbert or Austin's own brother who killed him! We're the only members left in town since the war."

"I'm left in town," Mead said blandly. "I might have killed him."

"Sweet of you to volunteer," Diane drawled, and went back to her deck chair. "Wake me up when you change the subject."

"Listen," Mead shouted at Phillips, "Austin wasn't robbed; the motive was a personal one. Somebody who knew him killed him. We knew him better than anybody. One of us killed him."

"Ridiculous!" said Phillips. "Personally, after I passed the time of day with Austin, I left the park and walked straight home. It would have been impossible for me to have murdered him."

"You could have come back." Mead smiled wickedly.

"Are you questioning my honesty?"

"Yes," Mead said, and rocked with laughter. His merriment goaded his friend into a burst of righteous anger.

"And what about you?" Phillips snapped. "How is your alibi?"

Involuntarily, I spoke up. "Oh, I'd have seen a wheelchair go up the hill, I mean ..." I floundered in painful embarrassment. Mr. Mead smiled at me and took my hand in his.

"Now, now, girlie," he said, "I know I can't walk. The doctors told me years ago. But, by Jupiter, Jove and Jiminy, I don't need that for an alibi!" He swung his chair away from me. "Penny, tell Phillips that ... Penny!"

Her father's shout startled the girl out of her self-imposed coma. Her eyes darted around the room as if she were trying to discover, exactly, where she was. A smile, apologetic and flustered, broke the grim line of her mouth. "I'm sorry," she said. "What did you say, father?"

"You were with me in the park this afternoon. You're my alibi. And I'm yours. Right?"

Penny laughed at him gently, softly. "A fine alibi you are for me. You were sound asleep about the time the Commodore was killed."

"I deny that! You make me sound like an old woman, dozing in the sun!"

"Nevertheless it's true. I can alibi father, but he can't me. Do I need an alibi?" She answered her own question and there was surprise in her voice as she did. "Of course, I do, don't I? It just never occurred to me that I might have killed Austin. But I might have, I ..."

"Another volunteer," Diane murmured. "Poor me, I feel so out of this."

"Father is out of it," Penny said. "I never left his side. I'm his alibi."

"The hell with alibis!" Mead exploded. "Motive! That's the thing, eh, Troy? Austin was a rich man. Richer than Phillips or I, and that, boy, is rich! Phillips, you probably know Austin's will. What about it?"

Phillips cleared his throat, the chairman of the board about to make a financial report. "I happened to have witnessed Austin's will. His estate is divided evenly between his brother and his nephew, Carl Marshall, Austin's late elder brother's son."

"Oh, yes!" I said. "Jeff met him this afternoon. He appeared just after the murder."

"Is that so?" George Mead leaned forward in his wheelchair. "Well, now, that's interesting. Carl was in the park this afternoon. Carl inherits a pile of money. Carl needs money. Carl ..."

"Father!" Penny cried.

"Carl always needs money! That profligate, good-for-nothing playboy, how he ever got into Uncle Sam's Army! But if he fights Hitler the way he fought with his uncle Austin ..."

Penny was on her feet, her eyes flaming anger. "Father, be still! You're accusing Carl of murder! You hate him, yes, you do! You know I love him. ..."

Mead snorted. "You don't love him! No daughter of mine would ever love a low character like ..."

"Carl is none of the things you say he is! He was fond of his uncle. He doesn't care about money, that's why he seems like a spendthrift. He certainly would never murder for money!"

"What," Mead bellowed, "was he doing in the park this afternoon? That, I suppose, was a coincidence, eh?"

"Carl was there," Penny said, and you could see her shoulders squaring for a fight, "because he was going to meet me."

George Mead sat slowly back in his chair and regarded his daughter with wounded disbelief. "You promised me you would never see him. And you've been seeing him every chance you get ... behind my back!"

"Yes, I see him! This afternoon while you were asleep I sneaked away to meet him at the Seventy-second Street entrance. And that's what Carl was doing in the park! Not killing his uncle!"

"And I suppose you'll marry him behind my back! You'll disgrace your father and ..."

"Now, now," Phillips said, "this is no time for family bickering." A slow malicious smile twisted his lips. "George, if Penny left you alone while she went to meet Carl, there goes your alibi!"

"No!" Penny's face went white, her eyes flew to her father, then back to Phillips. "No, I only left father for a few minutes. Carl wasn't there when I ..." Her voice snapped off abruptly and she raised the back of her hand to her mouth.

"Penny," her father said sternly, "forget about giving me an alibi, forget about your precious Carl's alibi. Tell the truth."

Penny swallowed. "Yes. I was to meet Carl at two-thirty, but I got there a few minutes late. He wasn't there. I was afraid something had prevented him coming and I couldn't wait because you might wake up. So I went back to you. I wasn't gone more than fifteen minutes."

"Those," Phillips said, "were fifteen vital minutes. It was about two-twenty that I talked with Austin. And I understand that he was killed within ten minutes after I left him." He paused, tugged nervously at his ear, then spoke again. "I hate to say this, Penny, but neither you nor your father has a valid alibi. And Carl, unless he can prove that he didn't arrive at the park until after his uncle's death, has no alibi either."

"I know he can prove it!" Penny cried. "Haila! Haila, you don't know Carl, but did you see a boy in a uniform go up to Austin?"

I shook my head. "Penny, I didn't see anyone at all go up that hill after Mr. Phillips talked to the Commodore. Nobody saw anyone. The police have proved to their satisfaction that nobody *did* go up that hill."

"Somebody did," Phillips said dryly. "Austin is dead … murdered."

"But in hell's name, how?" roared Mead. He spun his chair around to Jeff. "How, Troy? You haven't said a word since you got here! Speak up!"

Jeff grinned. "A word wouldn't have had much of a chance in this jam session. Not even edgewise."

"Come, boy, now's your chance! Ask questions, probe, detect! How else do you expect to solve this case?"

"I don't expect to," Jeff said. "I came up here to see if you had given me the thousand dollars. I want to return it."

"What, Jeff?" I asked hoarsely. "What did you say?"

"I want to return the money and … Haila, sit down over there. You'll be all right in a second." He pushed me into a chair and turned apologetically to the others. "It isn't that my wife is money-mad. She's just tired of selling papers, singing in the subways for pennies, stealing empty bottles to get the refund, things like that. Haila, do you want a glass of water?"

"Troy," Mead demanded, "why won't you take this case?"

"Because," I said too loudly, "he's a …"

"Haila!" Jeff interrupted. "Remember we're in mixed company. Wait till you get me home."

"Oh, no!" Diane said. "Haila, tell us what he is right here and now. Use vile epithets, I love them!"

"Now, now, Diane," murmured her husband. "Mr. Troy, seriously, I don't understand your attitude. A thousand dollars, after all, is not to be sneezed at."

Everyone was looking at Jeff, waiting for an explanation. Embarrassed by all the attention, he shoved his hand through his hair. "I'm not sneezing at the thousand dollars," he said, "I mean … it's this way. I don't think I can solve this murder. I don't think it will be solved. By anyone."

"Nonsense!" Mead exploded. "You can solve this crime, boy, I know you can! Have at it, boy, have at it!"

"No, thanks," Jeff said. "I hate to disillusion my wife, but there are a few smarter men in this world than her husband. Abbott and Costello, for instance, and Leo Durocher. And the murderer of Austin Marshall."

"More nonsense!" roared Mead. "Only stupid men get themselves into a position where murder becomes necessary. Troy, if you tried to …" He stopped and shouted at his daughter who was surreptitiously slipping toward the door. "Penny, where are you going!"

The girl didn't answer. Breaking into a run, she darted out of the room. The suddenness, the furtive intensity of her flight was startling. She ran as if for her life. Her father, infuriated, bellowed helplessly after her.

CHAPTER THREE

"Mr. Mead," Jeff said, "I'll tell Penny you want her." He grabbed my hand and towed me along at his side. "Good by, Mr. and Mrs. Phillips. So long, Mr. Mead."

Once outside the room, Jeff slowed to a normal walk. He had used Penny's exodus merely as an excuse for his own. We were halfway down the wide, thick-carpeted hall that split the huge, sprawling apartment when we heard the slam of elevator doors in the foyer. Behind us we could still hear the surging voice of Penny's wounded parent. The butler, alarmed by the noisy ado, came scurrying out of his pantry. He clutched gratefully at Jeff's casual request for his hat as proof that nothing really serious had happened.

By the time we reached the ground floor and the street Penny was, of course, out of sight. "Jeff," I said, "that girl's in trouble."

"If she's in trouble it's a family affair. The Mead family, not the Troy. Let's go see if Austin's brother slipped me that grand. I won't be able to sleep if it's in the house."

"If it *isn't*, I won't be able to sleep."

"Isn't there some ironing you could do?"

"Jeff, look at it this way. Murderers should be brought to justice. It's your duty as a citizen of the world to rid the world of …"

"Do you want to wait outside, Haila?"

"Outside of what?"

He nodded at the great, high stone house that took up half of the next block. It was one of those monuments that the millionaires of the nineties raised in seeming competition with each other. The Marshall brothers' father, or whoever was responsible for this house, deserved at least a medal of bronze. His castle was one layer of arched windows, balconies, cornices and gables piled upon another. The effect was medieval, austere; looking at it you could almost smell the oxen roasting in the fireplace. As for me, give me our little fireplace on Gay Street and a marshmallow.

Jeff stepped off the curb and started toward the Marshall mansion. For a moment, not wanting to witness the Troys' return to poverty, I hesitated. Then I saw across Fifth Avenue, raising its gloomy peak above the park wall, the knoll where Austin Marshall met his death. A chill started at the back of my neck and fluttered down my spine with a message to my legs. I followed my husband.

A moment later we were being requested by an elderly, weary-looking maid to wait in Mr. Austin's study for Mr. Bernard. The study, on the ground floor, was a large room, but even then it seemed to be higher than it was long or wide. A feeling that I was standing in a well came over me, a well lined with a million books. Jeff moved along the shelves, reading the titles.

"Austin," he said, "wasn't a one-hobby man. Not only model yachting, but ballistics ... philately ... numismatics ... cryptography ..."

"Huh?" I asked.

"To you, Haila, guns, stamps, coins, decoding."

"He would have to know decoding to figure out what the rest of his hobbies were. Decoding ... that's a strange hobby."

"Maybe he did counterespionage work in the last war."

In a corner there was a tremendous workbench and on it I saw a half-finished model of a Viking ship. The ship that was to have been the Commodore's present to his friend, Chuckie Clancy. I crossed the room for a better look and, as I did, a voice rose into audibility. It was Penny's voice, alarmed and urgent. The sound of it carried through an open casement window behind the workbench and overlooking what seemed to be a courtyard.

"The police are going to ask you questions, Carl," she was saying. "Tell me why you didn't meet me this afternoon. Where were you?"

A young man's voice answered her. "All right, Penny. I was off being a good Samaritan. While I was waiting for you I saw one of my uncle's playmates having what looked to me like a heart attack. I went to his rescue and I helped him home."

"Who was it, Carl?"

"Phillips. He was pretty damn sick."

"William Phillips? But he ..." Her voice trailed off in her surprise.

"So you see, I didn't kill my uncle." The young voice was grim. "I was taking Phillips home when it happened. We clear each other." There was a moment's strained silence, then Carl said, "Penny, don't you believe me?"

"Yes. Of course I believe you, but ..." Again the words dragged to a thoughtful halt. I knew what she was thinking.

Austin Marshall had been murdered within ten minutes after Phillips had talked to him. During those ten minutes Phillips had been taken ill and had been with Carl. There was his alibi, a perfect alibi. And yet William Phillips had refused to offer it.

There was a click and the study was instantly filled with a blaze of overhead light. I turned to find Bernard Marshall framed in the doorway, his hand on the electric switch beside it. His round, fat face looked strangely incongruous with the subdued expression it wore, and his eyes were troubled.

"I like lots of light," he said quietly. "A phobia of mine … darkness. You were admiring my brother's handiwork, Mrs. Troy?"

"The Viking? Yes, it's beautiful. It must have taken hours and hours to make."

"Yes. Austin wasted more time in his life than …" Bernard checked himself and stood silent, looking vacantly at the ship.

"Your brother seems to have had a lot of hobbies," Jeff said.

Bernard Marshall nodded. "All of these," he said, waving an arm toward the book-lined walls, "all hobbies of his. And he was a master at all of them. He spent his whole life …" He stopped and turned to Jeff. "You wanted to see me?"

"Yes," Jeff said. He stated the reason for our visit: the mysterious thousand dollars.

"No, I didn't send it." The fat man grimaced sardonically. "I have never seen that much money in my life, not all at once. My brother held the purse strings in this family and held them with a stranglehold. He was a possessive person and I've always been one of his household fixtures. All his life he kept me handy. I played with him as a child; I've been playing with him ever since. Hobbies … ships, coins, cryptography, trains. God, how I …"

Again Marshall checked himself; he pulled his plump hand across his eyes, and once again he became the man who had entered the room, calm and self-contained. He said softly, "I was fond of my brother. He was strange, but …"

"He was strange … period."

The words came from the young lieutenant who strode into the room. His eyes were very blue in his young, tanned face. Rugged and gallant in his uniform, he might have stepped out of a recruiting poster. This, then, was Lieutenant Carl Marshall and sufficient reason, it seemed to me, for Penny to incur all her father's wrath. She had evidently beat a hasty retreat for home, however, to keep that wrath at a minimum.

"Hello," Carl said to Jeff. "Nicer seeing you now than it was this afternoon."

"Carl," his uncle said, "did you hire Troy to solve Austin's murder?"

The lieutenant wrinkled his forehead. "How could I hire anybody? What's this all about?" He shook his head vigorously as Jeff explained. "No, I didn't do it. In fact, I'm glad you're not taking the case. I'm afraid you might prove that I had murdered Austin. To keep him from disinheriting me."

"Don't say things like that," Bernard said sharply.

"Why not? Everyone knows about it. Austin threatened to disinherit me once a month. It was a ritual that we both enjoyed. He never meant a word of it."

"That's true, but you talk too much. It's talking that gets you in trouble with everybody. With George Mead and ..."

Carl smiled. "That old lion hates my innards. Just because once I hid a little time bomb in one of his ships. The thing blew up ... right in the middle of the lake! He was going to turn me over to the F.B.I. Sabotage, he said. Bernard, you remember."

His uncle permitted a smile to flicker over his face. Then, abruptly, he said, "If you'll excuse me now ..."

Jeff jumped to his feet. "I'm sorry to have bothered you at all, Mr. Marshall. But I knew you wouldn't see me if ..."

"I'm glad you dropped in, Troy." Bernard shepherded us into the hall. "I needed someone to talk to. Someone who would forget the things I said as soon as I had said them. And forget the things Carl has said, too. Carl is not ... well, Carl is very young."

He turned and moved toward the great central staircase and started to climb it as his nephew walked with us to the door. Suddenly sobered, the young man bid us a quiet good night and then followed his uncle up the stairs.

As Jeff and I walked through the quiet night to the bus stop I said hopefully, "Darling, I guess you're going to have to keep that money after all. It's a shame, but ..."

"There's still Tony Gilbert."

"Where would an actor get a thousand dollars? I hate to have you earn so much money, dear, but it looks inevitable."

Jeff glanced at his watch. "Tony's in the middle of a performance now. I'll pay him a visit around eleven."

"As, Jeff, you still won't …"

"Sweetheart, listen …"

"Don't touch me, don't speak to me! And after I come back from Reno, don't keep trying to get in touch with me!"

"Haila, if you went to Reno I'd miss you terribly."

"Really, darling?"

"Yes. Can't you get a divorce here in New York?"

By the time we reached Gay Street the silence in our family had reached the screaming point. I hurried down the steps into number 39.

The woman was standing very still, letting the blackout darkness of our vestibule lose her in its shadows. I didn't know she was there until my hand brushed against the wooly softness of the cape she wore. Even then her face was but a blur of white, without shape or features. But I knew the voice instantly; the low throaty drawl was unmistakable.

"I've been waiting to see you," Diane Phillips said. "May I come in?"

Jeff was fumbling for his keys, trying to sound more cordial than surprised. "The moment I get this door broken down our house is yours. Anything you don't see, ask for."

Diane's voice smiled faintly in the darkness. "You're so kind. I've been waiting hours, it seems."

She followed us through the hallway into our living room, stood tall and quiet and poised while I snapped on a few lights. Then she moved to a chair and, crossing her long, gleaming legs, leaned easily back. Now I could see that the sultry, indifferent mask imprinted on her face was fraying at the edges. There was a tenseness about her, a sharp excitement, that she couldn't quite conceal. It showed itself in the too careful way she drew off her long suede gloves and lit a cigarette, in the too casual way she flipped her alligator purse onto the table at her side. But her voice remained languid as she turned to Jeff.

"Mr. Troy … Jeff, you're wrong. Austin Marshall's murder can be solved. And you can solve it. I've heard about you."

Jeff looked at her silently for a moment. "Mrs. Phillips," he said, "you ..."

"Diane," she corrected.

"Diane, you sent me that thousand dollars."

"Yes." She leaned forward suddenly, eagerly. "You see, I have faith in you! I know that you can clear up this horrible affair! I want you to accept the money and do just that ... name the murderer of Austin Marshall."

"Why?"

"Why?" The expensive eyebrows arched in surprise. "But that's obvious! Killers should be ..." She stopped and smiled. "Oh, I see. You want to know my ulterior motive. You're quite right; I do have one. I don't like the poking and prodding of the police. I want their questions to stop as soon as possible. They annoy me."

"Diane, I know the cops on this case. They're practically gentlemen. Their nuisance value is not one thousand dollars."

"You don't believe me!"

Jeff smiled. "Sorry."

She stood up and walked to the window. Her back to us, she gazed out into our dark little garden for a long moment. Then a deep breath raised her shoulders and head; she turned to Jeff. The mask had been dropped from her face in that interval. There was no sophisticated aloofness on it now, no boredom. There was only surrender, a kind of feminine helplessness.

Swaying ever so slightly, she went to Jeff and sat beside him, her right hand drifting to the divan's back just behind his head. "Jeff, please," she said. The low, provocative voice trembled under the weight of its appeal. "Jeff, you must help me, you must."

When she leaned toward him, her eyes wide and moist, her full red lips parted delicately, I rose quietly and slipped into the kitchen. Not because Diane's act was more than I could stand, but because I, worse luck, knew my man. Jeff, the softy, was a sucker for that dirty, female trick. In a minute, without my inhibiting presence, Diane would have him promising to track down Austin Marshall's killer to the ends of the earth.

But my cooperation went only so far. I mixed three drinks,

making much more noise than necessary to remind Diane that Jeff had a wife handy, a wife who was very quick on her feet and a helluva good infighter.

Diane's voice, now at the breaking point, ebbed lower. "I don't know where this horrible thing will end … you must help me, Jeff, I have no one else to turn to. I'm so terribly alone … and I'm frightened … frightened. …"

The pause that followed made me step quickly to the kitchen door. My husband and home meant more to me than several thousand dollars. Over Jeff's shoulder I saw Diane's face. She was closing in for the kill. Her lips were atremble, down each cheek coursed a beautiful big tear. Jeff flipped a handkerchief from his hip pocket. He blotted up one tear, caught the other as it swept down to the point of her chin. Suddenly her eyes hardened and her lips snapped shut. Jeff was laughing at her.

Diane stood up.

"All right," she said, "all right. We'll make this a strictly business proposition. One thousand dollars. Take it or leave it."

"I'm sorry, Diane, but …"

That settled it. Steps had to be taken, and I took them. Running to Jeff, I flung myself upon him. "Jeff, darling," I wailed, "you must help Diane, you must solve this murder! We need that money, we can't go on …" I put one hand behind his neck and pressed my head up under his chin. With the other hand I reached into his inside pocket and, with a skill that astonished me, extracted the envelope which contained the thousand dollars. I slipped it inside my blouse. "Jeff, I can't go on living from hand to mouth any longer! I can't …"

"Haila!" He took me by the shoulders and pushed me out to arm's length. "Haila, what's the matter with you?"

"Nothing. Forgive me." I went to the window and gazed out into the garden as Diane had done. "Forgive me, I … I've had a busy day."

Jeff's laugh was embarrassed. "Too much murder, I guess. It's a good thing I'm not taking this case."

"If that's final, Mr. Troy," Diane said icily, "my money, please. May I have it?"

"Of course!"

Jeff reached into his inside pocket. His mouth opened and closed; he swallowed. He did his vest pockets next, then all of his coat pockets, including another hand-dive into the inner one. Frantically, he rushed through his trouser pockets. His face kept changing from ashen white to a flaming crimson. My heart bled for him, but I steeled myself.

At last he managed to speak. "I've been robbed!"

"Ridiculous!" Diane snapped.

"It … it's gone! Haila, did you see it?"

"You wouldn't even let me touch it!"

"It's gone," Jeff said. "Gone."

"Oh, dear," I moaned. "It'll take us years to pay Diane back."

Diane was smiling. "You owe me one thousand dollars, Jeff. Find Austin's murderer and we'll call the debt paid."

"Oh, no!" I said, "not if Jeff doesn't want to. I'll get a job doing something. Scrubbing floors or something."

"I'll work on the case," Jeff said. "I'll work on the case."

"I'm so glad," Diane said, her eyes glinting. "Thank you and good night."

While Jeff saw her to the door, I crept into the kitchen. I put the envelope into the tea canister, pushed it down deep and buried it in the dry green leaves. It would be safe from Jeff there practically forever; he hated tea. I was back in the living room, sitting on the divan, when he reappeared.

He was rummaging dolefully through his pockets as he came in, shaking his head incredulously. He saw me watching him and stopped. "Damn it!" he shouted, "it's nearly nine o'clock … why isn't dinner on the table? I work hard all day and come home and there isn't any dinner on the table!"

"You didn't work today, darling, and you invited me out for dinner. Would you like some eggs?"

"There probably aren't any in the house! If I managed my business the way you …"

"There are a dozen eggs, dear."

"A dozen eggs! Six measly eggs apiece …" He stopped shouting and started to laugh. I laughed, too. "What the hell are you laughing at?" Jeff snapped at me. He sank down into a big chair and morosely looked a hole in the carpet.

After approximately ten minutes, I said, "Darling, money isn't everything." He didn't answer me. I tried again. "Dear, we have each other." That failed to cheer him up. The obvious thing to do was to curl up in his lap and playfully rumple his hair. But I was afraid for my life. Then I saw Diane's alligator purse on the little table. It might start the Troys speaking to each other once more. I held it up.

"Diane forgot her bag," I said.

"I declare," said Jeff.

"Some people," I said, very conversationally, "would forget their heads, if they weren't fastened on."

"Necessity," Jeff said, "is the mother of invention."

I went into the kitchen and began breaking eggs into a bowl. The telephone rang. "I'll get it, darling," I called.

It was Diane.

"I just discovered your purse," I told her. "We'll take good care of it …"

"Yes." She cut me short. Her voice was an urgent whisper. "Haila, something has just happened. I've got to see Jeff, I've got to tell him the truth. …"

"We'll be here all evening," I said.

"No! No, I can't go out of the house. They're waiting for me, Haila, they're waiting outside …"

"Who is?"

"I don't know. I only know I'm in danger. Please come at once … 26 Beekman Place … hurry. …"

"Yes, Diane."

"And, Haila! Don't ring the bell! There's a key in my purse, use it. I don't want my husband to know … he mustn't know anything about this! Nothing! Hurry, Haila, hurry, please!"

CHAPTER FOUR

AT THE corner of Christopher and Gay Streets we found a taxi. We rode to within a half block of our destination. There we reconnoitered by casually strolling the length of Beekman Place arm-in-arm, like lovers hoping that this gorgeous September night would never end. We saw no one lurking in the shadows of the quiet street, no one furtively watching number 26, spying on Diane. In fact, we saw no one at all; Beekman Place was deserted.

The Phillips house was in the middle of the block; it was tall and elegant and very superior, looking down its white granite nose at the more modest houses on both sides that refused to give it elbow room. Four iron-railed steps swept up to a double door. Above the door a half-circle of window tossed a fan of light on the pavement, but the windows on either side of it and on the two floors above it were dark. At the top of the building a crack of light edged drawn shades.

Jeff slid Diane's key into the lock and half of the heavy door moved smoothly, quietly open. We stood in a foyer that was mirrored from ceiling to floor. A crystal chandelier and a vase of waxlike lilies on a glass table repeated themselves indefinitely in the reflecting walls. I turned a slow circle. I saw a couple of hundred Troys, no one else.

We ventured through a slender arch into a room at the right. I saw the silhouette of a floor lamp, moved cautiously through the twilight and switched it on. This was a living room. I could imagine Diane seated on the long settee leaning graciously across the antiqued glass coffee table to greet her guests, to make them feel at home. At the moment I could have stood a little of that. I felt very far from home.

My eyes were attracted to a lamp table; a thin, final spiral of smoke curled up from a crushed cigarette in a tray. Jeff saw it, too.

He called softly, "Diane."

A moment later he called again, raising his voice just a trifle. "Diane." Still there was no answer.

I turned to step back into the foyer and saw our shadows cast weirdly on the wall behind us by the floor lamp. That was just the touch I needed. I stayed where I was and kept my eyes on Jeff. When he noticed that I was looking at him, expecting him to do something, he smiled reassuringly at me and sat nonchalantly on the settee. He patted the seat beside him.

"Sit down, Haila."

"I'd rather stand. Jeff, what are we going to do?"

"What are you whispering for, Haila?"

"You're whispering. Let's get out of here."

"I'll try calling Diane again. Shall I?"

"Well, do something."

"Diane!"

"Louder, Jeff. I couldn't hear you."

"Hey, Diane!"

This time there was an answer. Not a voice, only the breath of one. It came from the room in back of this, a faint, choking sound. We went rapidly toward it, through a door into a darkened room. Even before Jeff located the light switch I knew that this was the library. There was a musty, leathery smell about it.

The overhead light flashed on and sent my eyes reeling. Book loaded walls came first into focus, then red leather furniture, an oaken refectory table, a tremendous desk. Then I saw Diane. She was directly in front of me, almost at my feet. Her long slim figure sprawled grotesquely on the floor, one arm bent under her. Her black hair had come loose and it spread itself out wildly around her white face.

Before my knees touched the floor at her side she had moved. Her lashes fluttered and her wide eyes were staring blankly up into my face. She moved her lips but for a moment no sound came from them.

I said, "Don't try to talk, Diane."

"I'll be all right, I ..."

Her dazed mumbling ceased as comprehension leaped into her eyes. She shook my hand from her shoulder and struggled up to her knees. "Haila," she whispered, "did you see him?"

"Take it easy," Jeff said. "We didn't see anyone."

"He's still here!" She scrambled to her feet, her eyes darting about the room, searching every corner of it. "He must still be here. ..."

"Sit down, Diane, you ..."

"I heard you at the door, I heard the key in the lock just as he hit me! He must still be here ... somewhere in the house ... don't let him get away. ..."

The desperate urgency of Diane swept us into motion. I trailed after Jeff as he ran through the big dark house, switching on lights and trying windows as he went. Down a narrow staircase to the basement, through a pair of empty servants' rooms and the gleaming white enamel of a kitchen and its pantries. Up past the first floor again, up to the second. Through Diane's apple-green beruffled bedroom and the mirrored dressing room that adjoined it. Through a stiff mahogany bedroom that was William Phillips' and a Colonial guest room. Through more dressing rooms and baths. Climbing the last flight we landed in a garret-like room. Old chairs and tables, a huge roll-top desk, a carpenter's bench that was stacked with papers and magazines and strewn with parts of model ships and tools.

From the depths of a chair beneath a bridge lamp William Phillips rose, the book in his lap tumbling to the floor. His eyes behind their thick glasses blinked at us in sleepy amazement. He brushed his hand clumsily through his sparse hair. It took a moment for him to become his pompous self again.

"To what," he sputtered, "do I owe this unexpected visit?"

"Somebody," Jeff said, "just finished trying to deprive you of a wife. We found her lying on the floor in the library ... knocked out."

The man's mouth worked convulsively, but nothing except a jargled "Diane" was audible. He was almost to the door when Jeff stopped him.

"She's all right, Mr. Phillips."

"But she's down there alone, isn't she? Whoever attacked her might …"

"No. The house is empty. And locked. I gather this is the help's night out."

"Yes. We have a married couple and they always take …" Phillips removed his spectacles and then replaced them meaninglessly. "I … I don't understand. You've searched the house, you say?"

Jeff nodded. "Every door and window is locked from the inside. Except the front door, and no one could have gone through that without Haila and me noticing."

"The roof?" I said. "Could he have …"

"No," Phillips said, shaking his head emphatically. "You can only get to the roof through this room. No one came through here. I'm certain of that. I was merely dozing."

"No one in the house," Jeff said, "and no one went out of the house."

"That seems to be the case," Phillips said.

"But your wife was hit over the head," Jeff said, and waited. It took Phillips a second. Then his jaw dropped and he gaped at Jeff angrily.

"Surely," he gasped, "you are not implying that I attacked my wife!" The sallow complexion of his face exploded into a mottled red. "That's ridiculous, Troy, insane!"

"Haila didn't do it; I didn't do it."

"But why should I, *why?*"

The voice came from behind us. Diane was standing in the doorway, her black hair streaming around her shoulders, her makeup a shambles. But she spoke quietly and with control as she moved toward Jeff.

"But really, Jeff," she said, "how can you have such an absurd thought? If nothing else …"

"Diane, dear!" Phillips hurried anxiously to her side. "You're all right? You're certain?" She nodded and patted his arm, then faced Jeff again.

"If nothing else, you're accusing William of stupidity. And William isn't stupid. If he had attacked me, he would have left a window open to prove it had been an outsider. An outsider who escaped."

"I don't feel," Phillips said, "that it is even necessary for you to defend me, Diane. That I would attack you is ... is beyond even contemplation. I think Mr. Troy owes me an apology."

"I apologize for contemplating it," Jeff said.

Phillips shot him a sharp look. "I might question your sincerity, Mr. Troy, but I won't ... just now. Diane, what did happen to you in the library? Tell me."

"Yes, I will. Could I please have a cigarette?" Jeff handed her one and lit it for her. "Thank you. I was ... I was sitting in the library downstairs. I hadn't turned the lights on because I wanted to rest there just a moment before I climbed the stairs. I heard a movement behind me, then some instinct made me duck." She pressed the palm of her hand tenderly against the side of her head. "Unfortunately, I didn't get completely out of the way. I saw nothing of my would-be murderer before everything went black. The next thing I knew the Troys were with me."

"You didn't catch even a glimpse of the man?" Phillips asked.

"No, William."

"That's regrettable ... regrettable," he murmured.

"William, it was dark!" Diane flared. "How could I possibly ..."

"I'm not blaming you, my dear. Don't excite yourself."

"I'm not excited! Why should I be? I was merely smashed over the head, nearly murdered! Minor things like that don't excite me ..."

"Now, dear, now, now. ..."

Diane jerked her head impatiently, but she didn't answer. She walked into the alcove of a dormer window and she walked right out again. She patted her husband on the sleeve of his smoking jacket. He smiled at her, a mixed smile that was part forgiveness, part victory.

I looked uneasily at Jeff. For some reason that I couldn't quite understand I wanted to get out of here. Before I could catch his eye, Phillips was clearing his throat and saying, "Who could possibly have done this thing?"

"The murderer of Austin Marshall," Diane said. "That seems obvious. It can't be a coincidence that he was murdered and I nearly murdered on the same day, can it?"

"But, my dear, why should Austin's killer try to harm you?"

"I don't know. That's what frightens me."

"Being frightened does no good, my dear."

Diane's face tightened and she took a short, quick breath. Then she relaxed and said with what might have been a mock demureness, "You're right, William. Being frightened does no good at all. Jeff, what do you think? This … tonight is connected with Austin's murder, isn't it?"

"I'd say so."

"And I'd expect you to say so, Mr. Troy," Phillips said. "It seems to be a habit of yours to say the first thing that enters your head."

Diane said quickly, "William, I'm sure Jeff isn't even considering the absurd possibility of you attacking me any more! Why, how could you have? You were up here in your den. I saw the light as I came home."

"Yes, I've been here ever since dinner."

"But, William, whoever hit me must have been hiding in the house when I came in. Did you hear anything … anything at all?"

"No, I can't say I did."

Jeff said, "It doesn't look as if we're going to discover how Diane's pal got out of the house. But if we knew how he got in, we might get someplace."

"Yes, there's that." Diane dropped her cigarette on the bare floor and turned her foot on it. "But there again … well, he *couldn't* have got in! I mean the doors are always locked, the windows are never open … we have air-conditioning. Of course, he came in somehow but …" She lifted her hands in a gesture of bewildered defeat.

"I'm afraid," said her husband with a humorless indulgence, "that I know how any number of people could get into this house."

He picked up Diane's smashed cigarette from the floor and dropped it into a wastebasket. "My wife," he went on, "has a habit of leaving her infernal keys everywhere. I gave up changing locks years ago."

There was surprise in the quick look Diane gave her husband. Then, instantly, it was gone. She said eagerly, "Yes! Yes, I'm always losing keys! That's how he got in, I'm sure of it!"

"It's possible," Jeff said. "I think it's a safe bet, just as you say, Diane, that Austin Marshall's killer is the same person who attacked you tonight. You know lots of people Austin knew, you probably know his murderer. Have probably been in his home ..."

"And lost one of my keys there," Diane finished.

"Sure," Jeff said, "it's perfect. So perfect that I don't like it."

"Naturally, you don't," Phillips said acidly. "You have stated your preference. You prefer to think that I struck my wife. That was your first thought and you ..." He stopped and that pleased, superior smile wrinkled his thin lips. "Mr. Troy, tell me, how does it happen that you and Mrs. Troy found my wife? How, may I ask, did *you* get into my house?"

"William, we should be grateful that Jeff ..."

Phillips interrupted her rush of words to repeat his question. Diane's eyes were on Jeff, pleading with him not to give her away, begging him to evade her husband's question.

Jeff said, "I'm glad you asked me that, Mr. Phillips. I came up here to see you."

"To see me?" He was surprised and disconcerted. Diane relaxed; she leaned against the workbench and, pretending to equal her husband's surprise, said, "To see William? But why?"

"To ask him about the murder. There's something ..."

"Nonsense!" Into one word Phillips jammed enough indignation to inspire a lynching. "There is nothing about the murder that I ..."

"William," Diane said gently, "we must help to solve Austin's murder. What is it you wanted to ask, Jeff?"

"Why, when your husband has a perfect alibi for the time of Marshall's death, did he refuse to give it?"

Diane turned slowly to face her husband. The look she gave him was a worried question.

"Don't know what you mean," he muttered. "No idea what you're talking about."

"This afternoon," Jeff said, "after you talked to Marshall and were leaving the park, you became sick … faint. Carl Marshall saw you; he helped you home. Carl was grateful for that alibi which eliminated both of you from all suspicion. It removed you from the scene of the crime at the time of the crime. But you refused to even mention it. Why, sir?"

For a moment Phillips faltered and when he spoke his voice was unnecessarily loud. "It slipped my mind somehow. The excitement, you know, the impact of the tragedy … see here, Troy! By what right do you question me? By what right do you come barging into my house and …" His voice, which had risen to a shout, now dropped as he switched from the defensive to the offensive. "You haven't told me yet why you happened so conveniently to be in my house to find my wife. And you haven't told me how you managed to get in."

This time Diane came to her own rescue. She stumbled forward and caught at the back of a chair. She said weakly, "William, I … I'm afraid that I … that blow must have … I've got to lie down. …"

He was at her side. "Lean on me, Diane. Let me get you downstairs and I'll call the doctor."

"No, doctor, please! I only need rest. You can let yourself out, can't you, Jeff? I … I'll need William."

She was taking no chance that William might repeat his question concerning the why and how of our entrance into his house. She was still determined to keep her employment of Jeff a secret from her husband. Well, it was her thousand dollars, she was the boss.

As we left the house I realized that her reason for hiring Jeff was still a secret, too. Would Diane, I wondered, have told us the truth about that if her unknown assailant hadn't changed the evening's subject, or would her busy little mind have whipped up a batch of lies?

We turned right on Beekman Place. There were other questions I wanted to ponder aloud, but Jeff's face was set in a contemplative silence, that "Do not disturb" sign was hanging on his nose. I held my peace. The sooner he solved this case, the sooner I could confess my heinous crime and put the thousand dollars back in his pocket. I had just seen what happened to girls who kept secrets from their husbands, and I didn't like what I had seen.

I had followed Jeff onto a crosstown bus, off the bus and down Sixth Avenue to Fifty-first Street before I knew where we were heading. The Colony Theatre was pouring its audience out into the night; Tony Gilbert would be in his dressing room wiping the glamour from his face with cold cream and Kleenex. There was method in Jeff's meandering.

CHAPTER FIVE

Twice in my non-meteoric career as an actress I had played the Colony Theatre. The first opus, written by an unknown author, had run all of six performances. The second, by a well known writer, had run five performances. That had proved conclusively to me that fame meant nothing and that I could do without it.

So when Jeff came along and one evening, dancing to divine music in an air-cooled nightclub without a cover charge, began a sentence with the word "Will," I hastily shouted, "Yes!" not taking any chance that the rest of his sentence might not be "you marry me?" Jeff later claimed that the rest of his sentence was going to be: "you please take your foot off my right foot and put it on my left foot for a change?" I knew, of course, that he was kidding.

"Darling," I said, as we walked down the stage door alley, "you really were going to ask me to marry you?"

"Huh?"

"I mean, if not that night, eventually?"

"I hope Tony Gilbert isn't entertaining the Tony Gilbert Fan

Club. I'd like us to be alone with him. Oh, yeah, Haila. Sure. At least, eventually."

Jeff held open the stage door for me and we walked into the vestibule. There was a bulletin board, a dressing room key rack, a door leading onstage and the beginning of the staircase that rose to the dressing rooms. There were three high school girls, one with an already open notebook, telling an old man that they had an interview arranged with the lady star. The old man shooed them toward the lady star's room, then he looked at me and said, "Well, well, well. If it isn't the little girl herself!"

"Hello, Nick," I said, "you're looking fine."

"I am fine! Did you hear about Tim? The doorman at the Regent? Had to retire." Nick chuckled, delighted. "Too old."

"How old are you now, Nick?" I asked.

"Eighty-one."

"You lie, Nick! You're not a day over seventy-five."

He chuckled again. "I'm only seventy-three. But don't tell anyone. Say, I read about you in the paper! Discovered a body up in Central Park today! Now, is that the way for a young girl to act? On a Sunday, too. Why doesn't your husband keep you home?"

"He was with me. And he's with me now. This is Jeff, Nick. What's your last name, Nick? I never can ..."

"I couldn't tell you," the old man laughed. "Haven't heard it for so long. I even call myself Nick. Say, the police were here tonight while I was out for a bite. They talked to Gilbert. Tony Gilbert, he's a member of that yacht club, you know."

"Yes, we know," Jeff said. "The police didn't talk to you then, Nick?"

"Not yet. What would they want to talk to me for?"

"Well, the murder was committed between two-twenty and two-thirty. You'd be the logical one to establish an alibi for Tony if he has one."

"Why, sure, Tony has one. He came in here about quarter to two, ten to two. We talked a minute, then he went up to dress."

"Could he have got out this door again and back in without you seeing him?"

"I never left my chair here, sat right here until the performance started … no, sir, wait a minute." Nick grinned, slapped his knee and said, "Bless me, I am eighty-one! I did leave here, and you know why I did?" He chuckled. "Fellow came in here with a pressing job he done on one of Tony's costumes. He was in a hurry and I took it up to Tony's room for him. Tony must have been visiting in one of the other rooms. He wasn't in his. I hung up the suit and …"

Jeff said, "You know for a fact that Tony was in one of the other rooms, Nick?"

"No. But where else would he be? He didn't come down here, I'd have seen him."

A flock of white ties and low necks blew in. They demanded, in that hysterical midnight manner of people about to spend a lot of money at a big name café for a very little fun, to see Maggie. The lady star's first name was Mary; they called her Maggie for short. Nick ignored them until he had answered Jeff's question, told him the number of Tony's dressing room.

The actor greeted us as if he had known us for a hundred years, but hadn't seen us for fifty. His cordiality made me almost expect to see a picture of Jeff and me stuck in his makeup mirror. When he waved us into straight-backed chairs, he turned them into feather-stuffed divans. Tony's friends weren't fooling when they said he gave his best performances in his dressing room.

"I take it, Jeff," he said, "that you're going to solve Austin Marshall's murder."

"Just like that," Jeff said.

Tony stripped off his costume, that of a private in Uncle Sam's Army, stood for a moment in his shorts as he hung up the uniform, then slipped into a frayed old dressing gown. All this without batting an eye in my direction, and me a lady. The theater was a wonderful place; informal.

"A policeman named Hankins," he was saying, "dropped in to see me before the performance this evening. He inquired after my alibi."

"How is your alibi?" Jeff asked.

"Fine, thanks." He sat down before the mirror that was surrounded by wire-basketed bulbs and attacked his makeup. "Nick, the doorman, can tell you that I got to the theater a little before two. While Austin was being murdered, I was right here in my dressing room. If I'd gone out again, Nick would have seen me."

"And he didn't see you go out again," Jeff said.

Tony laughed. "Oh, you asked him already?"

"You know me, I'm shrewd. So at the time of Austin's death, you were here."

"That is correct."

"You didn't leave your dressing room at all? Not to visit one of the other actors, for instance?"

"Are you accusing me of speaking to other actors, Troy?" Tony put up his dukes. "Step outside. Haila, hold his coat. No, Jeff, seriously, I didn't budge out of here."

"So," Jeff said, "it looks like you have an alibi."

"And am I proud of it! It's my first alibi! It just goes to show … this is indeed the land of opportunity. Ten years ago I came to New York empty-handed. And now I've got a job, a bank account, three charge accounts and an alibi!"

"Good alibis are hard to get nowadays, Tony. Take good care of it."

"Oh, I will! I'll keep it in a cool, dry place."

Jeff got up and roved over to the clothes rack. "You wear the works in this part, don't you, Tony? Everything from fatigue to when the President pins the medal on you. Say, this blouse looks as if it had just come back from the presser."

"Yeah, I sent it out after the show last night," Tony said absently. He was deeply involved with the makeup around his eyes.

"When did the presser return it?"

"I don't know. It was here in time for the matinee today and that's all that …" He swung away from the mirror and faced Jeff with a puzzled grin. "Is this a rib? What's funny about a guy getting his clothes pressed?"

"I'll tell you," Jeff said, smiling. "See if you don't think it's hilarious. Nick brought your blouse up here … after you had arrived at the theater. You didn't know that because you weren't here. You weren't out visiting in one of the other rooms. You didn't go down the stairs or Nick would have seen you. Where were you, Tony?" Jeff wagged his finger at the actor. "Were you hiding in a can of cold cream or ..." He broke off and sauntered over to the room's one window and leaned out. "A fire escape. And a supple lad like you could use it ... in and out ... and not be seen. It's ten minutes or less to the lake from here in a cab ..."

"Aw, shucks!" Tony snapped his fingers. He was laughing. "My nice alibi! Haila, your husband is ..."

"Don't misunderstand me," Jeff said. "I'm your pal, Tony. Hankins is going to talk to Nick. He's going to find out what I have."

"That's right, thanks, pal. Hankins is going to wonder if maybe I didn't beat it back to the park and do in the Commodore, isn't he?"

"That's what Hankins gets paid for."

"So I'll have to cook up another alibi."

"Yeah. And on the spur of the moment, that would be tough. Why don't you try a new one out on me? So you'll be ready for Hankins."

"Oh, I hate to put you to all that trouble, Jeff!"

"No trouble at all, really, old man."

"Awfully good of you. Now, let's see. I think I'll use a woman."

"A very good thing to use," Jeff said.

Tony stopped smiling; his face became grave. "Surprisingly enough, this is the truth. I skipped down the fire escape, not to be surreptitious, but because it's a short cut, and I met a lady. We strolled through Times Square together."

"Pretend I'm Hankins," Jeff said. "Gilbert, why did you come up here first? Why didn't you go directly to meet this lady?"

"Because I had been sailing in Central Park and I wanted to wash up before meeting this lady. And that's the truth, too. What's getting into me?" Tony was grinning again. "It isn't like me to sit around telling the truth!"

"What's the lady's name? All Hankins has to do is to check with her."

"There's my complication," Tony said. "That's the reason I cooked up my phony alibi. Because when Hankins would ask for the name of the lady for checking purposes, I would refuse to give it to him."

"Oh. The lady has a fair name which shouldn't be dragged into a murder case?"

"The lady has a husband," Tony said.

"I'm sorry," Jeff said.

"She's sorry, too. But the old dog has dough; I haven't. She loves me, but love isn't everything. Money is. She's so crass. And so beautiful."

"Who is she, Tony?"

"Oh, no, pal!"

"Her phone number would do."

"No. Spelled N–O."

I said, "Thanks, Tony."

The actor's perfect teeth flashed in a quick smile. "I'm protecting my interests, Haila, not yours. I bet your husband has a way with ladies."

"Not me," Jeff said. "The gleam in my eye is too obvious. Before I even step into a crowded elevator the women start screaming. Tony, Hankins, being an unromantic soul, is not going to accept that new alibi of yours without the lady's verification."

"I can see that. But I'm fond of that lady, mighty fond."

"So fond that you don't mind being a murder suspect for her sake?"

"Troy, you couldn't understand unless you saw this lady. And you're not going to see her; Hankins isn't going to see her. Just Tony is going to see her. And her husband occasionally, I'm afraid."

"Well, that's that," Jeff said. "How's your show doing, Tony?"

"It'll run another year."

"Like your part?"

"It's good enough. I'm on stage from beginning to end. I mean, even if I don't matter much, at least I'm there where the audience can see me." Tony slapped a piece of grease-laden Kleenex into the wastebasket. "Frankly, I hate the damn thing! Of all times to be a make-believe soldier! A wooden soldier! It makes me slightly sick at my stomach. Not," he added sarcastically, "that I don't give my all. You should see Gilbert giving his all night after night at the Stage Door Canteen. And the Merchant Seaman's Club. I'm a great big brave busboy. No tray is too heavy for Gilbert to carry, no tray too sticky for me to wipe! You should see me sneak up on an empty Pepsi-Cola bottle; they call me Commando Gilbert. Or you should see me heroically doing shows at the war plants and shipyards. I'm the stuff, I am."

"What's the matter with your leg, Tony?" Jeff asked. "I noticed the cane this afternoon."

"I've got one of those trick knees that folds up every once in a while. Football. Not to mention a trick ulcer. Highball." Tony was laughing again. "I'm a victim of America's favorite indoor and outdoor sports."

Jeff stood up. "Take better care of yourself, Tony."

"I'm glad you stopped in. I hate to be all alone when I take my own face out from under the greasepaint. Good night, Haila."

"Good night, Tony. Come and see us."

"I will, thanks. Let me know when your husband leaves town."

"Good night, Tony," Jeff said.

It had been a too, too busy day and when Jeff suggested that we head for home, I was grateful. It took all my willpower not to fall in bed with my shoes on. When my head hit the spot where my pillow should have been I was too tired even to snatch it from behind the neck of my thieving, reading husband. I couldn't be bothered ...

I was sitting on a rocky little knoll in Central Park. Below me on the bright blue lake sailed a thousand ships. My face had launched them. I was so beautiful, that's why I was going to be murdered. I knew it, but I couldn't move to prevent it. The thing was creeping closer ... up the hill it came ... through trees ... through park benches ... invisible to everyone but me. It was Bela Lugosi, it was Boris Karloff. Now it was Jeff pretending he was under contract to Hollywood's leading horror studio. There was a long sharp piece of steel in his hand. I heard the crunching sounds he made as he crept closer. I sat on the bench and waited ... waited with my neck ready ...

I awoke with a start. I was sitting bolt upright in my bed in the pitch blackness of the room. But the little sounds that had awakened me and saved me from a nightmare death were going on. They came from the back of the apartment where someone moved with a stealthy caution about the rooms there.

Reaching out my hand, I felt for Jeff's shoulder. His bed was empty. I tried to call him and my voice came out in an unrecognizable squeak that made me jump. Stage-whispering his name brought no response. The shuffling noises were approaching the bedroom now. I scrunched down deep under the covers.

"Jeff!" I howled with all my might.

His voice came from right inside the bedroom door.

"Haila, be quiet, I …"

A slamming door broke off his words. There were pounding footsteps. Another slamming door, more footsteps in the hall outside. Then silence. After a lifetime I heard Jeff come slowly back into the apartment. He switched on the lamp and stood at the foot of my bed, glowering at me.

"If you hadn't opened your little mouth," he said, "I would have had him."

"Who?"

"I don't know. But I had him ambushed when you started yelling. And when I came back to quiet you, he got out."

"But what could he have wanted? What was he after?"

Jeff shook his head, puzzled. "Something in our living room. Or in the kitchen."

"The kitchen!"

I leaped out of bed. As I raced through the living room, I caught a fleeting montage of open, ransacked drawers, pillaged bookcases and upholstery, pictures upside down. In the doorway I stopped, afraid to even look. I forced my eyes past the open stove drawer, the upset breadbox, to the row of bright-painted canisters on the shelf. The lid was off the coffee canister, the flour, the rice, the sugar … and the tea. I lunged to it and thrust my hand inside. There was nothing there, nothing but tea.

I didn't have to turn around to know that Jeff was watching me from the door. I got a grip on myself; I shook the tears from my eyes. I said, "Well! This is a pretty mess! A girl tries to keep her house as neat as a pin and then someone …"

"What could he have wanted in here?" Jeff asked.

"I … I wouldn't know," I said. Then the tears welled out of my

eyes and poured down my face in a torrent. I found myself wail-
ing like a bereft banshee. Jeff took me in his arms. "Don't cry,
darling. Mrs. Clancy will clean up tomorrow ..."

"We can't afford Mrs. Clancy any more," I sobbed.

"Why?" Jeff asked sharply. "What do you mean?"

"I ... I don't know what I mean. ..."

"You go to sleep, Haila. Just go to sleep."

I tried to, but how can a girl who has just been robbed of a
thousand dollars that she stole from her husband get any sleep?
Crime doesn't pay, and criminals do not rest easy; I found that
out when the first light of morning came creeping through our
windows and I lay still awake, twisting and turning in step with
my writhing conscience. Jeff was sleeping like a baby; I could
have kicked him out of his bed. Now I knew why the Dillingers
and the Jameses hated the police so much.

CHAPTER SIX

THE ringing of the telephone awakened me. Rubbing the night
out of my eyes, I groped my way through the devastation that had
been my living room before some son of a cyclone had vandal-
ized it and pillaged my tea canister.

"Hello," I said, and a voice said: "Jeff."

"Just a minute, I'll get him."

"Haila, *this* is Jeff."

"Oh. Hello, Jeff."

"Aren't you up yet? It's two o'clock in the afternoon!"

"Monday afternoon?"

"Yes, sweetheart."

"You needn't be so patient with me, Jeff! It doesn't necessarily
have to be Monday afternoon, does it?"

"Well, no. But yesterday being Sunday sort of makes the odds
against it being Tuesday overwhelming. Why are you so testy,
darling? Not to mention irritable?"

"You'd be testy and irritable, too, if you could see this living room!"

"Get out of it, Haila. Look, I'm at the studio now. Do you want to meet me at Austin's park bench in an hour?"

"I could think of more pleasant places to meet."

"Maybe the murderer stole that thousand bucks out of my pocket and if we find the murderer ..."

"I'll meet you at the bench, Jeff."

"And then we'll have lunch at the Zoo Cafeteria. So long, Haila."

"So long."

I did just enough to the living room and kitchen so that Mrs. Clancy wouldn't think my husband had come home drunk and spent an hour or two swinging me around by my hair. I threw away the tea. Perhaps Attila hadn't washed his hands before snatching our money. I made myself slightly presentable and was ready to go.

The weekend having drawn to its murderous end, Central Park was once more in the hands of the children, and the air was shrill with their screaming laughter. The lake was dotted with their boats, not so large nor so expensive as the grown-ups', but just as colorful. A parade of baby carriages, piloted by white-uniformed nurses, encircled the big blue lozenge of water. Balloon men and candy men and park attendants, tall as Gullivers in Lilliputia, threaded their ways through the crowd of New York's small fry.

As I walked toward the knoll I could see Jeff's solitary figure atop it. From my audience point of view he looked like an actor on a slightly tilted stage; no lethal-minded person could have approached him unnoticed. The semicircle of the knoll that faced me was a rocky terrace split by a path of concrete steps. The far side ended in a thirty-foot cliff, a smooth, steep drop. Even if someone had miraculously managed to scale that height I should have seen him as he clambered over its brim.

"Jeff," I said, as I arrived at his side, "no one but an invisible man could have murdered Marshall. Hankins is right; it didn't happen."

"Yeah," Jeff sighed. "The more I look at this place the more discouraged I get." He sat down on the bench and gazed morosely out across the lake. I started to sit beside him and quickly changed my mind. Jeff didn't have the squeamish sort of imagination I did.

I said, "Remember Bolling's theory? That it might have been done from a distance?"

Jeff grunted unenthusiastically.

"That thing *must* have been fired from some sort of a weapon. It had to be, didn't it?"

At first I thought he simply hadn't bothered to answer me. Then I saw that he was watching something with interest on the lake below. My eyes followed his; they landed on a little black schooner that bobbed merrily across the water. I had seen that ship before; I knew its name. It was the Smuggler.

My eyes traced the Smuggler's course back to its point of departure, and I saw him instantly. He towered over the children who swarmed around him, his black hair ruffling in the breeze, the malacca stick twirling jauntily in his hands. Obviously yesterday's tragedy had not dampened Tony Gilbert's enthusiasm for model yachting.

"Look," Jeff said.

"At Tony, you mean?"

"At his ship."

The Smuggler was nearing the concrete wall across the lake from Tony. Watching it, I saw an almost perfect repetition of the scene I had witnessed twenty-four hours before. A young woman in a tweed suit and a canary-yellow beret crouched at the water's edge, waiting for the schooner to pull into port. Her hands moved out to it and swooped it from the water, saving it from a crash landing. Straightening up, she held the ship at arm's length, examining it with admiration. Then, cradling it for just one second in her arm, her hand disappeared into the tiny hold. Almost in the same motion, she returned the Smuggler to the water, reset its sails, and sent it on its homeward journey.

"Jeff!" I exclaimed, "she took something out of Tony's ship!"

"Yeah, I think she did."

I glanced back at Tony Gilbert. He was down on one knee now, a child crowded in on either side of him as he adjusted the mast of a toy sailboat. He was completely oblivious, or pretended to be, of his Smuggler's adventure.

Jeff said, "Isn't that the same girl who picked up Tony's ship yesterday?"

"She's the girl who tried to pick it up. Only Austin Marshall beat her to it."

The girl was walking away from the lake's edge toward a bench on which lay a small green boat. She sat down beside it and leisurely lit a cigarette. She exhaled a formidable cloud of smoke, then her head moved slowly as her eyes swept the expanse of water and shore. Her glance flicked past Tony with no sign of recognition as he busily worked on the child's ship.

I said, "Tony doesn't know what she did, Jeff."

"He doesn't seem to, does he?"

The young lady carefully ground out the briefly smoked cigarette under her heel and rose. Swinging the green sailboat by its mast, she sauntered along the walk away from the lake.

"Let's go," Jeff said. "Casually."

We went down the rocky crag and followed the woman to the Fifth Avenue corner. Her saunter had given way now to a purposeful stride. Her yellow beret bobbed along in front of us like a bright bouncing beacon.

She crossed Fifth Avenue, went down it four blocks, then turned east, walking faster and faster. At Madison Avenue I was winded. At Park I was gasping. When the woman turned into the entrance of a brownstone house near Lexington, my lungs croaked their gratitude.

The brownstone was a one-family house. As if he knew what he was doing, Jeff breezed up to the door and rang the bell. My qualms at his aggressiveness hadn't had time to materialize before the door swung open and the woman stood looking at us with a half-smiling inquiry. She held the yellow beret in her hand; her curly, red-brown hair was charmingly mussed. Her lips and cheeks glowed with a pale baby-pinkness and she wore no makeup at all. Her thick eyelashes were gold-tipped.

"How do you do?" Jeff said cheerfully.

"How do you do?" she said, and waited.

"This is my wife," Jeff said. "The reason she's so out of breath is that you walk too fast. I'm glad you don't live any farther from the park."

"You followed me?" Her blonde eyebrows jerked in surprise. "But why? You sound like a ... like a detective."

"Ignore the noises I make, they're deceptive. But I have, unfortunately, been trapped into investigating the murder of Austin Marshall."

"Oh? Yes, I read about the murder."

"You were in the park yesterday. I thought you might be able to help me, Miss ..."

"Mrs. Mrs. Davisson. I don't know why you think I can be of any help. I didn't know Austin Marshall. Ours was a mere nodding acquaintance. I've never seen him except at the lake. However, if there's anything I can do, Mr. ..." Mrs. Davisson smiled. "Now it's your turn."

"Troy. Jeff and Haila Troy."

"Come in, Troys."

We followed her into a large sunlit room, gay with bright chintzes and bleached furniture and bowls of flowers and leafy plants. The green sailboat was on the mantel, another larger one stood beside it. It was a nice room, as natural and healthy looking as the woman who lived in it.

She had lighted a cigarette and perched herself on the arm of a low divan. She expelled one of her clouds of smoke.

Jeff said, "You don't inhale, do you, Mrs. Davisson?"

She laughed. "Have you a theory that Mr. Marshall's murderer doesn't inhale?"

"I have a theory that your husband doesn't allow you to smoke. And that your cigarettes are smuggled to you by an actor named Tony Gilbert."

"What *are* you talking about?" She punched out the cigarette at once. "Tony Gilbert ... who is he?"

"Tony is the master of a model schooner called the Smuggler. Yesterday you tried to intercept it but Austin Marshall beat you to it. Today, having no competition, you were able to pick up the Smuggler. You ..."

"I love ship models! I've been sailing them for years! Unfortunately, I'm not clever with my hands, so I must buy my models. And when I see a beautiful job like the Smuggler, I can't resist it! I have to pick it up and look at it."

"Mrs. Davisson, you're very clever with your hands. The way you took something out of Tony's ship would have made a magician jealous. And it wasn't cigarettes, of course. That was my whimsy at its most elephantine."

The woman eyed Jeff silently for a moment, then her laugh pealed out, a lilting laugh full of amused incredulity, too full of it. "What could it have been? Jewels, perhaps? Or the Mona Lisa? Or opium? You *are* whimsical, Mr. Troy, and I love it!"

"I promise," Jeff said, "that I will positively not breathe a word to anyone."

"About what?" she asked sharply.

"That you are connected in some mysterious way with Tony Gilbert, who is connected with Austin Marshall, who was murdered. I won't even tell the police. I'm not a good citizen."

"You mean, of course," Mrs. Davisson said slowly, "that you must tell the police. And then, what is actually a silly, innocent thing may become embarrassing ... and serious." She picked up a cigarette, regarded it and then tossed it back on the table. "I met Tony Gilbert last spring while I was sailing at the lake. Quite frankly, his charm overwhelmed me. We began seeing each other. We were always," she added with a special emphasis, "chaperoned by the other patrons of the nightclubs we met in or the other strollers on Fifth Avenue. Tony made it all such fun. He's an incurable romantic. He lives in a dream world, a stage world; he must dramatize everything. He decided that if my husband learned about us he would kill us both in his blind, jealous fury. In his mind he had my husband following us, spying on us. He wanted me to wear a veil ... that I refused to do. But when he suggested that we, for the sake of our lives, communicate with each other only via the Smuggler, I agreed. It's such silly fun!"

"So that's what you took out of the ship. A communication. Of a romantic nature."

"That's all. But, really, I must put a stop to it. Because of my husband." Her eyes crinkled and her merry laugh rang out again. "When I told Walter about it he was furious. Oh, not because he mistrusts me!" she added quickly. "But, you see, Walter is Doctor Davisson."

"Really!" I said.

"Huh?" Jeff said.

"Mrs. Troy, I see that you have tuned in on Station WQW at one o'clock, Mondays through Fridays. And, Mr. Troy, I see that you haven't."

"I'm sorry," Jeff said. "What is your husband's program?"

Mrs. Davisson smiled. "Is your marriage jeopardized? Going on the rocks, headed for disaster? If so, present your problem to Doctor Davisson. His keen analysis and sympathetic advice has saved countless marriages ..." She dropped the monumental tone of an announcer and said, "Walter is The Marriage Doctor."

"Oh," Jeff said.

"A great deal of it is silly ... corny, but a great deal of it isn't. Walter is made fun of, he makes fun of himself, but he does do good. He is a psychologist and his program is a fine opportunity for him. But! You can see what would happen if it became town gossip that The Marriage Doctor's own marriage was in jeopardy ... jeopardized by his wife's flirtation with an actor. Walter would be laughed off the air! So I promised him that I would stop this nonsense with Tony pronto. And he thinks I have, but somehow I ... I haven't managed it yet. I'm like a child with a dangerous toy ... I hate to give it up. I'm so very naughty. Mr. Troy, you wouldn't tell on me, would you?"

"No," Jeff said, "I wouldn't breathe a word of that story to a soul."

She raised her head sharply. "Do I detect an undercurrent in your voice, Mr. Troy? An undercurrent of disbelief?" Then she leaned back and was smiling again. "I shouldn't blame you. Two grown-ups sending notes to each other in toy boats. That is rather hard to take, isn't it? But how can I prove it to you? By my husband? That would be disconcerting, since he thinks I have dismissed Tony from my life."

"You could prove it to me by showing me the note. I love to

read other people's mail."

She looked at him frowningly; her teeth bit into her pale pink lip. "Oh, dear!" she said. "But, why not? After all, I'm not a blushing schoolgirl." Her hand darted into her sweater pocket and came out with a crumpled slip of paper. She glanced at it, shook her head ruefully and passed it to Jeff. "I'm afraid I'm going to blush after all. Please don't read it aloud."

Jeff held the note so that I could see it over his shoulder. It was written on light blue paper in a tiny, studied script. "Marjorie, darling," it said, "it seems centuries since we were last together. It was a wonderful day, remember? We fed the pigeons in the park and watched the roller skaters at Radio City and walked to the East River. Don't fail me this Thursday. I'll be waiting for you in the lobby of the Algonquin … Thursday night at nine-thirty." It was signed merely with a "T."

Jeff looked up and grinned. "Don't bother blushing, Mrs. Davisson. It sounds more like propaganda to see New York first than a love letter."

"That's because you can't read between the lines, thank heaven!" Smiling good-naturedly, she extended her hand and took back the letter. "And now you believe me, Mr. Troy? I won't be embarrassed by the police?"

"You may rest assured. Only one more thing. Was there a note in the Smuggler yesterday when Austin Marshall intercepted the ship?"

"Yes. Tony was terrified that Marshall would find it. Fortunately, he retrieved the Smuggler in time."

"You're sure of that?"

Marjorie Davisson nodded. "Tony told me when I saw him just before his matinee yesterday."

"Do you know that he refuses to give himself an alibi for the time of the crime in order to save your honor?"

"Yes, I know. He called me last night. He promised me that Gestapo methods would not force my name from his lips. Of course, if Tony's chivalry should get him in trouble with the police, I shall have to intervene. But in the meantime, let him have his fun with his dramatic sacrifice."

"Knighthood," Jeff said, "is still flowering."

"Charming, isn't it?" Mrs. Davisson glanced at her wristwatch. "Please forgive me, but I'm going to have to be rude. I'm expecting my husband home any minute now and if he found you here … well, one thing would lead to another and …"

"Walter would spank you for not chasing Tony away," Jeff said. He rose and reached for his hat. "We should go anyway. There is work to be done."

"There is eating to be done," I said. "I'm famished."

"I don't know, Haila," Jeff said doubtfully. "Diane called me this morning. We have to be at 26 Beekman Place at five …"

"We have an hour almost!" I insisted. "Don't be cruel!"

"Is your husband cruel, Mrs. Troy?" Marjorie Davisson said with mock solemnity. "Does he beat you? Present your problem to Doctor Davisson … but don't tell him I sent you! Good by, Troys. Good luck."

CHAPTER SEVEN

My tray loaded to the gunwales with the Zoo Cafeteria's wonderful beef stew, salad, rolls and butter, plus a dish of chocolate ice cream for Jeff, I joined him on the sunny terrace that overlooked the seal pond. He pointed at my tray.

"What's that, Haila?"

"Beef stew."

"Are you sure? Taste it."

"What are you talking about, Jeff?"

"There's a beef shortage, you know."

"I know. Well?"

"As we passed the aoudad cage, did you see the aoudad?"

"Jeff, be quiet! I paid forty-five cents for this stew and I want to … oh, look! There's Penny Mead and her soldier boy over there in the corner."

"Yeah, let's join them."

"Oh, no," I objected. "We don't want to crash a rendezvous!"

"Some rendezvous. I never saw a stonier silence. It's our patriotic duty to blast it. C'mon, dynamite, and don't spill your aoudad."

Penny and Carl Marshall did seem to welcome our intrusion. In fact, they seemed much happier to see us than each other. In exactly ten seconds, with startling frankness, Carl was telling us the reason for his and Penny's mood indigo.

"Please," he said, "tell Penny to marry me."

"Penny," Jeff said, "marry Carl."

"Thanks, I will," Penny said. "But not today."

"It's a beautiful day!" Carl said. "Your father won't roar any less another day. Penny, this damn marriage license is burning a hole in my pocket. Haila, you talk to her. I'm sure your father couldn't have agreed to your marrying Jeff."

"I was smart," I said. "I didn't let my father see Jeff until after we were married."

"See, Penny!" Carl said. "Lots of people elope. It's the safe and sane thing to do."

"Jeff and I didn't elope exactly. We met each other in New York and got married here. Then we sent wires to our families announcing the wedding."

"And, Haila," Penny said eagerly, "what was your family's reaction?"

Jeff laughed. "Haila's father sent me a wire: 'Understand you have married my daughter. Thanks.' "

"You see?" Carl said. "What else could your father do, Penny?"

"Carl, please." Penny looked ready to cry. "It isn't just father, it's … well, your uncle …"

"Darling, I'm not being heartless about Austin … but my leave is up soon, only five more days now! Penny, marry me! Marry me right now!"

"I don't know, I …"

"You're afraid of your father!"

"No! No, I'm not! He couldn't get any more furious about my marrying you than he does about my sneaking away to meet you."

"Sneaking away to meet me," Carl repeated. "Penny, are we going to do that forever?"

For a long time Penny didn't speak. She sat there, just looking at Carl. Then she turned her eyes away. "Can you imagine what it's been for a man like father to spend eleven years in a wheel-chair? Father used to sail a real yacht, not a toy one. He used to hunt and fish … skiing, golfing, everything! He was a great ath-lete in school and he never stopped being one. Oh, I know! Why should I ruin my life by taking care of father …"

Almost angrily, Carl interrupted. "He doesn't need taking care of, darling! If your father thought you were taking care of him he'd hate it! You know that, Penny, it's true!"

"Yes, that's true, but it's … it's all so mixed up!"

"Penny, you *are* afraid of your father."

"Yes, I suppose I am. I don't know why."

"It's all inside of you, darling. It's silly! Your father isn't …"

"Carl! If you tell me his bark is worse than his bite, I'll … oh, let's not, Carl, let's not. I see you so little and then we fight." She turned brightly to Jeff and me. "Did you know that Carl and I are in love?"

"From a mile away," Jeff said. "Penny, is there any chance that your father will ever …"

"No. He'll never get out of that chair. His legs are paralyzed. It was a hunting accident. He and Austin Marshall were hunting up in the Canadian woods and Austin's gun went off accidentally. It was a spinal injury and …" Penny stopped. Before the fright that was gathering in her eyes had reached its climax, Carl had put his hand over hers.

"Penny," he said, "your father never held that against Austin. They were still friends … real friends. Don't think what you're thinking, darling."

"You're thinking it, Carl."

"Penny, it's … it's silly! She's being silly, isn't she, Jeff? How could George Mead have got up that hill? Let alone get up there without being seen? Besides, your father wouldn't … wouldn't … not Austin! They were like brothers! More than that … pals!"

"All right, dear, all right." She smiled wryly. "But I'm glad you're an engineer, not a criminal lawyer. I can hear you telling a jury not to be silly. How to win juries and … oh, lord!"

She leaped to her feet, snatching her purse from the table. I realized the reason for her hasty departure even before I looked. Through the archway that separated the bird house from the lion house plunged a streamlined, chromium wheelchair. George Mead's righteous indignation was evinced by his breakneck speed, a speed which sent pedestrians sidestepping for their lives. His great head jerked back and forth as he searched for his errant daughter.

"Stop him," Penny said anxiously, "please, stop him! Talk to him, Jeff, say you haven't seen me. Say that I'm probably back at the lake worrying about him ... say anything. ..."

She dashed back into the cafeteria and ran for the side exit with Carl at her heels. I followed Jeff down into the quadrangle and toward George Mead. He saw our approach and swerved to meet us. He started shouting at twenty feet.

"You, Troy! Have you seen Penny?"

"No, sir, not today."

The chair came to a violent halt before us. "She thought I was asleep, but I fooled her! Played possum for her! She sneaked away to meet that young scoundrel again! She's around here someplace, all right!"

"She's probably looking for you now, sir. Worrying about you."

"I doubt that! Penny never worries about anyone but that no-account young Marshall! They've got their heads together right now! Plotting against me, that's what they're doing! Out of my way, Troy!"

"If you'll just go back to the lake, sir ..."

"Out of my way, Troy, or I'll run you down!"

The outraged invalid zipped his chair around the seal pool and back out through the arch. He was much too irate to search meticulously for his daughter. Satisfied that he would soon locate Penny, without Carl, I suggested to Jeff that I have some coffee.

"Sorry," he said. "We have a date with Diane."

"Oh, yes, I forgot. Shall we take a cab?"

"Sure, one of those big nickel ones. Remember, Haila, that ..."

"I remember, I remember!" I said. Till my dying day that empty tea canister would stare me in the face and the footsteps of that contemptible unhousebroken housebreaker fading away with our treasure would ring in my ears. And all because I had deceived my husband, because I had sunk to pickpocketing …

"I still don't see," Jeff grieved, "how I could have lost that money."

"That's right! You did lose it, didn't you?"

"What do you mean, Haila?"

"Nothing … I was thinking of something else." Careful, Haila, I warned myself. It was Jeff who lost the thousand dollars; it wasn't stolen out of the tea canister. Bear that in mind, Haila, don't betray yourself. If your husband ever finds out what a rat you are … Oh, dear, I thought, this is the stream of a criminal's conscience, I've got to get a grip on myself. "Darling," I said brightly, "did you ever hear the story about the drunk who brought home a horse and …"

"Haila," Jeff groaned.

"Oh, I'm sorry, dear! You told me that one, didn't you?"

"Five years ago." He stopped walking, put his hands on my elbows and turned me to him. He looked into my eyes. "Haila, what's wrong with you?"

"I'm all right, darling, I'm perfectly all right, perfectly all … Jeff! Jeff, do you love me?"

"I told you that five years ago, too."

"And darling, no matter what happens you'll go on loving me?"

"Gee," Jeff said slowly, "maybe that *was* aoudad you ate."

I forced a laugh from my lips. "Yes, something has got into me, hasn't it? Aren't I being … what am I being? C'mon, we'd better hurry!"

All the way to Beekman Place Jeff kept glancing at me out of the corner of his eye. I pretended not to notice and continued small-talking away. At times the talk got so small it wouldn't have even filled a Hollywood gossip column. It was with delight that I climbed the steps of number 26 Beekman Place and rang the bell. Immediately the Phillips' butler blocked the doorway, one hand resting solidly on the partly opened door, the other on its frame.

"Mrs. Phillips," he said, "is not at home."

Jeff said, "You're expecting her though?"

"Mrs. Phillips," the butler said, "did not leave word when she was to be expected."

"But she asked me to call at five. She must …"

I saw a myriad of tall, gaunt reflections step into the mirrored foyer and it was a moment before my eyes managed to locate William Phillips in the flesh. He slipped smoothly into the position the butler had been guarding without leaving the doorway unbarricaded for a single second. His thin face wore a worried look, but his voice was as strongly cantankerous as ever.

"My wife left some time ago. She didn't say when she would be back. Why did you want to see her?"

"We were just in the neighborhood," Jeff said glibly, "and … I gather she's recovered from the attack on her last night? If she's out, I mean."

"Is that all you wanted to see her about … her health?"

"Well, I thought she might be able to tell me something more about that attack. Some little thing she might have remembered. …"

"Mr. Troy," Phillips said, "don't bother my wife. Don't concern yourself about her. I would be grateful if you stayed away from here. Thank you, Mr. Troy."

The door closed in no uncertain terms. And the snapping of a lock put a period on those terms. Jeff and I stood on the stoop, looking at each other.

"I wonder," I said, "if Phillips knows that you owe his wife one thousand dollars worth of work. And, if he does, would he still be so anxious for you not to work on this case, I wonder."

"I wonder, too," Jeff said.

He turned slowly, reluctantly, and went down the stairs. We hadn't quite reached the corner when there was a pattering of quick footsteps in back of us. A woman was running rapidly down the street. Under the coat thrown over her shoulders I could see the blue and white of a maid's uniform.

"Mr. Troy!" she called. "Mr. Troy!"

We walked back a few steps to meet her. She was more breathless than her short run should have made her, her eyes were bright with excited worry. The surreptitious glances that she shot back up Beekman Place made you expect to see someone, perhaps William Phillips, following her.

"Mr. Troy, she did leave you a message, Mrs. Phillips did." Her voice was the hurried whisper of an unwilling conspirator. "She can't see you in her house, it isn't safe there. She sneaked out and she's waiting for you now. You'd better hurry, Mr. Troy, she's there now, waiting."

"Waiting where?"

"McDonough's Bar and Grill." The woman looked pained. It was obvious that she considered McDonough's no place for a lady to wait. "It's on Third Avenue," she added, in even more pain. "Between Forty-eighth and ninth."

"We'll go there right away," Jeff said.

"Yes. Yes, right away."

Her eyes darted up and down the length of Beekman Place. Except for the lone figure of a man waiting in front of the bus stop at the corner and the three of us, the street was deserted. "Don't let anything happen to Mrs. Phillips," she pleaded, and then she slid back up to number 26 and scurried into the service entrance.

We walked westward to Third Avenue and located McDonough's Bar and Grill. It was a dark and narrow saloon wedged between a tailor shop and a store to let. Its unwashed window was filled with placards announcing cinema attractions of the neighborhood theaters for the past two months. Crepe paper streamers, all gray and tattered with age, formed a valance for the top half of the glass. A long skinny, gin-sodden-looking black cat lay on its back inside the window and swatted halfheartedly at some flies that buzzed above it.

I said to Jeff, "Not very attractive."

"Disgusting," he said.

"How Diane could go in a place like this ..." I said.

"How anyone could," Jeff said.

We pushed open the door and went in. An old battered bar ran the length of one wall. On that wall hung McDonough's hall of fame: pictures of Washington, F.D.R., Jimmy Walker, Harry Greb, Joe Louis, the 1927 Yankees, Betty Grable, and Betty Grable again. Your first reaction, after one glance at the back of the saloon, was to turn in a fire alarm. But it was only a jukebox, one of the more imaginative types that make Technicolor pallid and the Tri-Borough Bridge a catwalk.

The bartender stopped wiping his brow with the bar rag as we passed. "Hello, Jeff," he said.

"Hello, Arty," Jeff said.

I didn't say a word. I should have known. McDonough's Bar and Grill was within a mile of Jeff's place of business.

At one of the few tables in the rear sat Diane. A big black hat fringed with tiny balls drooped down over one side of her face. A swathe of silver fox curled around her neck and up the other side of her face. She was twirling an empty old fashioned glass between the palms of her hands. We slid into chairs at her table.

"Hello!" she said brightly. "I do so love this little place! The service is impeccable and the wine list ... ah, the wine list! Of course, the headwaiter must know you, I mean, but must practically be a member of your family!" Her voice was high and hard; she was a little bit tight. "Here comes the wine list now!"

Arty slapped a hand affectionately on Jeff's shoulder.

"The usual, Jeff?" he asked.

"The usual, Arty," Jeff said.

"And for the ... is it the little woman?" Arty asked.

"It is the little woman," I said. "And whatever the usual is, it's for me."

"I knew you'd marry the right type, Jeff," Arty said.

"Thanks, Arty," Jeff said. "How are things?"

"On Third Avenue," Arty said, "things don't ever seem to improve. On Second Avenue they tear down the El. A marked improvement. On First Avenue ..."

"Arty, if I may call you Arty," Diane said carefully, "one more old fashioned and that's all we'll be needing."

"Yes, ma'am."

It was plain that Arty didn't consider Third Avenue improved by Diane, her silver foxes, her Antoine coiffure, her Helena Rubenstein makeup and her Ilka Chase imitation of all that glitters. She waited until he had ducked back behind the bar.

"I wanted to have a confidential chat with you," she said. "This is much more confidential than Beekman Place. William came home."

"Yes, we found that out," Jeff said.

"He saw you! He knows that I made an appointment with you?"

"No," Jeff said. "Your secret is still intact."

"William mustn't know that I ... I hired you, that I wanted a detective!" Her long fingers beat a nervous tattoo on the table-cloth. "If he should find out ... wait!"

Diane lit a cigarette as Arty came to our table. He put an old-fashioned before Diane. Before Jeff and me he put the usual: a shot of straight whiskey and a small beer. There was so much whiskey that I felt qualified to ask: "Arty, which is the chaser?" This pleased Arty highly. He said, "Jeff, I knew you wouldn't go wrong and make a mistake as is more often than not done. Why don't the both of you drop in again some other time?" He picked up Diane's empty glass and carefully wiped the table in front of her, then he went away to serve a newcomer at the bar.

"Jeff," Diane said, "I haven't been telling you the truth. You knew that, didn't you? I haven't told you the real reason I engaged you."

"But you're going to tell me now?"

"Yes. I've got to. The police are getting close to it. They're going to find out everything soon. They've already had his valet at headquarters for questioning."

"Whose valet, Diane?"

She didn't answer. She was staring at the bar, the smoldering languor of her eyes expelled by an indignant "Well, really!" expression. It was directed toward Arty's most recently arrived customer, a compact little man in a gray hat so new looking it made the rest of his clothes seem faded. He was standing at the end of the bar near us and he was indulging in that time honored prerogative of all café habitués; he was eavesdropping. His ear seemed, literally, bent in our direction. He turned to learn the reason for the interruption in his entertainment and met Diane's withering glare. The little man flushed clear to the crown of his new hat, withdrew his head into his hunched shoulders and bent low over his beer.

Diane smiled and said, "He probably thought I was the floor show. Shall we move? My loud, raucous voice must be very annoying. Beer-curdling, in fact."

She swept up her big black purse and her gloves and led us to a table in the corner. Then, as if there had been no halt at all, she said, "Austin Marshall's valet. They took him to headquarters this morning. I haven't seen him, I don't know what he told the police. Nothing, I presume, or the police would have called on me. But I'm afraid the man will eventually tell what he knows. There's no reason why he shouldn't."

"What," Jeff said, "does Austin's valet know?"

She opened her mouth and then closed it. For a moment she looked as if she were going to make a break for it and run. Instead she leaned forward and took a deep breath. I could see now that she hadn't been drinking, not enough to matter. Her keyed-upness, her over-brightness grew out of her excitement. She clasped her hands together to keep them still. She spoke slowly.

"This isn't going to be easy ... this that I have to say, that I must say. Austin's valet will tell the police about Austin and me. He knows all about us. He would, of course. You see, Austin and I were in love. We had been in love for a long time. We hadn't done anything about it. But we were going to. I was going to divorce William and marry Austin. There. There it is."

Jeff said, "Does your husband know that?"

"No! No, he doesn't!" Her fingers pressed themselves white against the edge of the table and her voice was an urgent whisper. "You're thinking exactly what the police will think! That William murdered Austin! That he murdered Austin to keep me from going to him. But that isn't true! William never knew about us, never. You must believe that! The police won't believe it, but you must ... you're my only hope!"

"You hired me," Jeff said, "because you're afraid the police will hang the murder on your husband. You want me to find the real killer before ..."

"Yes! Before the police find out about Austin and me. And before my husband ..." She paused and then finished in a rush. "Before he is accused of murder."

"Diane, you were going to say before he finds out about you and Austin."

Her eyes dropped, but only for a moment. When she raised them she looked steadily at Jeff and she smiled. It was a little smile, and bitter. "Yes, and there's that, I'm afraid. William has never even suspected about me and Austin. And I hoped, if the case could be solved quickly enough, he might never … never need to know. Because, you see, it wasn't until after Austin's death that I realized …" She hesitated, the smile still twisting her lips. "I realized that I had never really loved Austin. When he died, I … I was sorry. That was all. I was shocked. But I didn't feel what I would have felt if I had loved him. That was the first time I knew how much William meant to me, and what I had done to him with my stupid romance. For years I've been taking William for granted. All my thoughts have been for myself, never for him. I never knew that until now … now when it's too late. Too late unless …"

"Unless," Jeff said, "I find the killer not only before the police learn about you and Austin, but before your husband does." He shook his head dismally. "I wish I could tell you not to worry."

Diane reached both hands across the table and grasped Jeff's arm. "You've got to help me," she pleaded. "It's my fault that William has a motive for murder. It's all been my fault from the beginning. I'll never forgive myself if …" She stopped, withdrew her hands. "You never saw me before yesterday. Why should you help me? You shouldn't … I don't expect you to, but …"

"Sure," Jeff said, "I'll try. I am trying."

"Thank you. If you need more money, let me know. I'll see if I can …"

"Let me see if I can earn it first."

"You will," she said quietly. "I'm sure you will. I think I'd better go now." She stood, but she waved us down. "Let me go alone. It's better that way. Wait a few minutes, please."

We watched her as she gathered her things together and walked out of the bar. She didn't walk with her long, lithe stride, her shoulders didn't have their usual disdainful swing. She moved limply. From the back Diane Phillips looked like an old woman.

"That was tough, what she did," I said. I took a good gulp of my drink. "That's what's called baring one's soul, isn't it?"

"More," Jeff said, "of a soul striptease."

"What more did you want? What more could she have told us?"

"She might have told us why someone is trying to kill her. Why she got hit over the head last night."

"But, Jeff, if she doesn't know …"

"That's right. If she doesn't know, she can't say. C'mon, let's get out of here, shall we?"

Arty must have been downstairs rolling out another barrel of beer, so Jeff tucked a bill under the ashtray. I followed him out of McDonough's Bar and Grill. He stood on the sidewalk, smothered in thought. I was tired and my feet hurt. That was why I took advantage of him and gently guided him into a taxi that we could ill afford. As I climbed in after him, I stretched back my hand to pull shut the door. My hand didn't touch metal; it touched a face. I squealed, flopped into my seat and twisted around toward the door. I couldn't see the face; all I could see now was the back of a brown coat as it eased itself into the seat beside me.

"Jeff!" I said.

"Hey," Jeff said, "this cab is taken, mister."

Mister slammed the door and turned to us. It was the little man at the bar with the new gray hat. He said, "Please forgive me, but I am desperate. I must speak to you." He leaned forward to the driver. "Take us through Central Park, just around in the park." He leaned back to us. "Please forgive me, but I am afraid that they are murdering my daughter."

CHAPTER EIGHT

"MY NAME," the man said, "is Robert Nichols."

He pulled up one of the folding seats and slid into it, his back to the door. Now he could look at Jeff without throwing himself out of joint. He took a blue silk handkerchief from his breast pocket and wiped his lips, then immediately licked them wet again and sucked them in between his teeth. His round, pale blue eyes blinked incessantly. His face seemed to writhe with worry and fear. Mr. Robert Nichols was in bad shape.

"Take your time," Jeff said. "Wait till we get to the park. Relax for a moment."

"This is very difficult for me, this situation. It was panic that drove me to intrude on you in this fashion. When I saw you about to go away ..." The handkerchief flicked over his mouth again. "I overheard you there in the bar room, talking to the lady. I gathered you were a detective. I hadn't thought of that ... of enlisting the aid of a private detective. And there you were, and I ... well, I was desperate. I can't go back to Dallas ... to Laura's mother and tell her that ... that she will never see Laura again. I can't do that."

Mr. Nichols turned his head and looked out the front windshield. The cab was crossing Lexington Avenue. When it had reached Park Avenue and swung north on it, he turned back to us. He was calmer now.

"I am a teacher in a small conservatory of music in Dallas," he said. "My salary is small and this trip has been a strain on me financially, but I promise to send you something every week until I have paid for ..."

"Tell us about your daughter," Jeff said. "What makes you think her life is in danger?"

Mr. Nichols was silent for a moment. "Mr. Troy, I can't answer that question in a sentence. I must tell you the whole story. I'll try to be brief."

"Don't be brief. Tell us everything."

"Yes. It ... it starts when Laura came to New York two years ago to ... to seek her fortune. She was always a restless, ambitious girl." He smiled wryly. "More like her mother than her father. At any rate, she got a job right away, a good job as a stenographer with a large insurance company. Her letters were triumphant and happy. She was living at a girls' club and everything was fine. That first summer she came home for her vacation. We had a wonderful two weeks together, Laura and her mother and I. That was the last time we saw her."

"But she wrote to you after that?"

"Yes. Yes, she wrote. When she came back to New York, for some reason that she never explained, she didn't return to her club. She took an apartment on Twelfth Street."

"By herself?" Jeff asked.

"She never mentioned anyone else. But then her letters never said anything, really. They were suddenly strange."

"In what way?"

"Well, she'd always written newsy letters to us, chipper and chatty. Now they were just a few lines saying that she was all right and that we were not to worry. Mother and I hadn't been worrying, but when she started telling us not to ... well, you know how parents are. And her letters grew more and more infrequent. Once, after not having heard from her for almost three weeks, Mother and I wrote to her in care of the insurance company. They sent the letter back with a note. Laura had left their employ; they knew nothing at all about her."

"When was this, Mr. Nichols?"

"Two months ago. We thought then that Laura hadn't found another job, that she was in need. We sent her some money ... to Twelfth Street. That letter was returned. She had moved from there and left no forwarding address. We were frightened then. We had the Dallas police report the matter to the New York Missing Persons Bureau. But nothing came of that ... they weren't able to locate Laura. Then, last week, a letter came from her. She had sent it to the conservatory; she didn't want Mother to worry. She begged me to come to New York immediately, to take her home. She was living in Hoboken ... number 479 Pine Street, Hoboken. There wasn't much else in the letter except ... except this: she said I was not to go to the police. 'Whatever happens, Father, don't go to the police.' That was all. I told Mother the conservatory was sending me to Chicago on business and I came to New York. I arrived this morning."

"You've been to Hoboken, of course."

"Yes," Mr. Nichols said, "I've been to 479 Pine Street, Hoboken. At noon today. I didn't find Laura ... she wasn't there. I talked to the woman who lived in the house. She had never heard of my daughter. I described Laura ... she had never seen her. She said that only she and her family lived in that house and that they had lived there for nine years."

"Could there have been a mix-up about the address?"

Mr. Nichols smiled unhappily. "If only there could have been! No. I got ahead of my story. As soon as I got off the train in Pennsylvania Station I got the phone number of 479 Pine Street from Information. And I called that number. I spoke to Laura."

Jeff slid forward on his seat. "You spoke to your daughter this morning! You're positive it was she?"

"It was Laura. I know my daughter, her voice, her manner of speaking. Yes, it was Laura. But we only talked for a minute, we were cut off. I tried to call again, I tried several times, but there was no answer. I went to the house then right away and ... I've told you what happened there."

"How much of the house did you see? Did you get upstairs?"

"Yes, I did. When the woman told me that Laura wasn't there, I ... I'm afraid that was too much for me. I became frantic. I nearly knocked the woman over and rushed up the stairs. In the hall on the second floor there was a man. I couldn't cope with him physically. He ejected me forcibly from the house." The little man's mouth straightened into a grim line at the unpleasant memory. "All I saw of the second floor were several closed doors. Laura was behind one of those doors, I know she was. I shouted her name. If she had been able to, she would have answered me. She wasn't able to, I know that, she ..."

We rolled the length of the reservoir, crossed the Ninety-sixth Street transverse, and the cab climbed into the countrylike end of the park at the north. None of us was looking at the other.

"The police," Jeff said. "This is for the police."

"I can't ... not quite yet, Mr. Troy. Not until the last resort. Laura was so explicit about that, so ... so urgent. As though her life itself depended upon it. Or perhaps," his voice sank to almost zero. "Perhaps there's something else. The trouble that Laura is in might be the kind that no one must ever know about. It's happened to girls before … against their will. Laura was an attractive girl, she …" Mr. Nichols stopped speaking; he closed his eyes.

"I'll go to Hoboken," Jeff said.

Robert Nichols nodded; he opened his eyes and they said the rest.

"Have you checked into a hotel?" Jeff asked.

"No. My bag is still at the station."

"We'll drop you off there. You get settled for the night and … let's see. Call me about midnight at our place. If I'm not back by then I will have called my wife and left a message for you." Jeff gave him our phone number and then told the driver to take us to the Pennsylvania Station.

It was an endless drive. Robert Nichols seemed to want to say more to Jeff, to give him more help, but all he was able to manage were abortive attempts at gratitude. The cab stopped on the Seventh Avenue side of the station. Nichols crawled out, then poked his head back through the window.

"Mr. Troy, you've got that address?"

"479 Pine Street."

"Yes. I'd better tell you how to get there. It's confusing. Right outside the ferry station in Hoboken, you take a number 14 bus. Get off at Kendall Street. It's about a fifteen minute ride. You walk up Kendall … it's a hilly street, walk up it two blocks to Pine. You turn left on Pine. The house is in the middle of that block. Will you repeat that to me, Mr. Troy? You mustn't have any trouble finding it."

Jeff repeated the directions.

"Yes," Nichols said. "I hope that … well, good luck. You'll be careful? Careful for yourself, I mean."

"Don't worry about me. There's one more thing, though. If I should find Laura and she … if she isn't well enough to speak to me … what does she look like?"

"She has curly blonde hair, her eyes are blue like mine. People have always said that Laura was the image of her father. If you find her, Mr. Troy, you'll know she's my daughter."

"All right, Mr. Nichols. You call us at twelve. Good by."

"Good by, Mr. Troy. And thank you, thank you again."

Jeff gave the driver our address. I looked back through the rear window. Little Mr. Nichols stood there on the sidewalk staring after us. My last glimpse of him was as he turned toward the station and moved uncertainly and slowly through the huge front doors. No matter what his mission, Robert Nichols would always look lost and defeated in New York, or any large, strange city.

"Jeff," I said, "why are we going home first? We could get a ferry at Twenty-third Street."

"I'm dropping you off at home. And I'll get the ferry at Christopher Street."

"But I'm going with you!"

"Not this time, Haila."

"Yes, Jeff."

"479 Pine Street doesn't sound like a safe place for young ladies," Jeff said.

"I want to help Mr. Nichols."

"You can help more by staying at home."

"Oh, all right. Whatever you say."

As our cab eased to a stop before our house, a man strode out of its shadows and opened the taxi door for us. It was Bolling, assistant to Lieutenant Detective Hankins of the Homicide Squad. We were not glad to see him; the murder of a wealthy model yachtsman seemed far away now and not very important.

Jeff paid the enormous taxi bill and set in motion the brush-off that would induce Bolling to come back another time. But the assistant detective was adamant.

"I just want to talk to you for a minute."

"Sorry," Jeff said, "but I have to go to Hoboken."

"Hoboken? Are you kidding? There's no reason for anybody to go to Hoboken."

"I've got friends over there," Jeff said.

"Oh, yeah?" Bolling was skeptical. "Well, if you do, you shouldn't have. Listen, Troy, don't pretend you're not interested in the Marshall case. I happen to know you been working on it."

"Did Hankins send you to see me?"

"Nope, I'm on my own. This is my night off. I got a theory about Marshall's murder. I wanted to talk to you about it."

"See you tomorrow, Bolling. These friends of mine in Hoboken ... well, I'm late now."

"You're going over there on the Marshall case. You know something Hankins and I don't. Listen here, Troy ..."

"This has nothing to do with Marshall. Bolling, it's your night off. Go to a movie." Jeff shook his hand. "Have a plate of vanilla ice cream afterwards. You deserve it."

"I don't like vanilla," Bolling said.

Jeff kissed me on the cheek. "I'll hurry home, Haila." He started walking down the street. Bolling caught his arm.

"Troy, I got a squad car across the street. I'll drive you over to the ferry. We'll talk on the way."

"All right," Jeff said. "Good-bye, Haila."

"Good-bye," I said.

I followed the two men across the street and climbed into the back of the car. When Jeff, in the front seat, turned his head and looked back at me, I said, "Just for the ride, dear. Bolling will bring me back home."

"With pleasure," Bolling said. He got the car under way. "Now, Troy, listen to me carefully. Are you listening?"

"Carefully," Jeff said. "Bolling, try to miss that cab there."

"I don't like cabs. Now, then. William Phillips talked to Austin Marshall at two-twenty. Your wife discovered Marshall dead at two-thirty. He was killed in those ten minutes. Correct?"

"Correct," Jeff said. "Bolling, the light's green. You may now safely cross Seventh Avenue."

"That's a funny shade of green," Bolling said. "Or is it my eyes?"

"Stop stalling. I've got to get to Hoboken."

"Now, where were our various suspects between two-twenty and two-thirty? Are there any valid alibis? Bernard Marshall, the victim's brother, admits he was still in the park. Furthermore, he was with himself ... I mean, alone, nobody to give him an alibi. The nephew, Carl Marshall, was near the scene of the crime. By his own admission, he was there waiting for a rendezvous, if I may put it that way, with Penny Mead. Carl is a likely suspect. Penny was alone in the park in those ten minutes, on her way to meet Carl at two-thirty. Therefore, she is a likely suspect. With Penny gone, her father, George Mead was alone. ..."

"Bolling," Jeff said, "don't stop at this street. The light is green."

"They ought to put them lights where a driver can see them. Therefore, Mead is a ..."

"A likely suspect?" Jeff asked.

"Undoubtedly," Bolling said. "Phillips talked to Marshall at two-twenty. But he was still in the park at two-thirty, at which time he ran into the nephew, Carl Marshall, and they left the park together. In those ten minutes, Phillips could have sneaked back and nailed Austin Marshall. Now, let us take up Tony Gilbert, who claims he was not in the park. He says he was with a woman in Times Square during the ten minutes. But he won't divulge the name of the woman, so his alibi is hardly valid."

Jeff was likewise refusing to divulge that the name of the woman was Marjorie Davisson and that she had validated Tony's alibi for us. Or perhaps he wasn't listening to Bolling; perhaps he was thinking of another woman, a younger woman named Laura Nichols.

Bolling stopped the car in front of the ferry station. He put a heavy hand on Jeff's arm to prevent his leaving before the summation.

"So," he said, "if you will add up the total suspects, you will see that we got six people who could have killed Marshall between two-twenty and two-thirty. Namely, Bernard and Carl Marshall, Penny and George Mead, William Phillips and Tony Gilbert."

"Bolling," Jeff said, taking the detective's hand off his arm, "you're right. That theory of yours is right; it holds water."

"But, Troy, I haven't told it yet!"

Jeff got out of the car. "Your theory, Bolling, is that we don't know who killed Austin Marshall. And you're right, so right. Good night, Bolling. Have Haila point out the traffic lights to you. 'Bye, dear."

" 'ByeThe only chance I get to do any thinking of my own is on my night off! And Troy won't even listen to me! Nobody will listen to me! Sometimes I wonder if it's worth the effort for me to think!"

In his chagrin, Bolling ground the gears almost to a powder, so he didn't hear me climb out of the car and push shut the door. I just made the boat. Jeff was as far forward as he could get; he was going to be the first ashore. I found a place where he wasn't likely to see me and I sat down.

Crossing the Hudson at night was usually fun. There was the Manhattan skyline, always a thrill. There were the big docks on both sides of the river and the big ships coming home or going away, and the barges and the tugs, and the other ferries taking care of the local trade. There were the boys and men in small boats who seemed to be daring the bigger craft to run them down. A lot to see and all of it fun.

But not on this night. Not when on one side of the river was a worried-to-death little man who had told us of a girl on the other side of the river. I wasn't enjoying this trip. I wasn't looking at the skyline or the big and little boats. I was keeping my eyes on the Jersey shore and wondering if we'd ever get there. I wasn't worried about what Jeff would say when he found me with him. I was only worried about Laura Nichols, too worried about her to sit at home and wait.

The ferry boat hit the piles and churned its way into the perfect fit of the slip. I was right behind Jeff when the gates went up. I followed him through the station and out onto the street. A number 14 bus was standing at the curb. We boarded it, Jeff and I. We dropped our fares into the box. We sat down simultaneously in a seat at the rear of the bus. Jeff looked at me; he took a deep breath and let it out slowly. He shook his head, not more in sorrow than in anger. Sorrow and anger were running neck and neck.

I said, "Darling, I won't be in your way! And you might need me. You just *might!* There's that possibility!"

"Haila," Jeff said. "Haila …"

"Haila what?"

"That's all. Just Haila."

"Secretly, Jeff, you're glad I'm here."

"Yeah, but I won't admit it. And if you get hurt, I'm warning you, I'll break every bone in your beautiful body!"

"And I'll hold myself while you do it! I'll have it coming to me."

"I won't need any help from you."

"Jeff, how do we know when we get to Kendall Street?"

He peered out the window. "My, but Hoboken is a dark place. I'd better confer with the driver." He was back in a moment; we would be notified upon our arrival at Kendall Street.

We sat there without speaking. The bus balked to an endless number of stops, passengers took an endless amount of time getting off and on. Now that I knew I was actually going to be with Jeff when he walked into number 479 Pine Street, things began to happen to me. Little things, like a feeling in the pit of my stomach, like wanting to smoke a cigarette more than smoking a cigarette was worth, like wishing the girl in the seat across from us would suddenly say, "I'm Laura Nichols, could you tell me where my father is?" But the girl kept on reading her book and the bus kept getting closer and closer to Pine Street.

I was afraid to ask Jeff how he meant to handle this. What he was going to do about the man who had forcibly ejected Mr. Nichols from his house, what he would do if there were more than one man and all of them didn't want Jeff to see Laura Nichols. I was afraid to ask him those questions because I was afraid he didn't know the answers himself.

"Hey," Jeff said, "how long have we been on this bus?"

"It seems like hours."

"It seems like more than fifteen minutes. That's what Nichols said it took."

Jeff got up and staggered through the lurching bus to the driver. I saw the man hit himself a self-abjurating blow on the forehead with the palm of his hand. Jeff motioned for me to join him. I did, and the driver told me personally how sorry he was that he had forgotten all about us and how he deeply regretted the fact that Kendall Street was three blocks to the rear. He said that he should be shot. Jeff told him that it was quite all right, that it didn't matter in the least. He convinced the driver that it was really a very charming thing he had done and that he certainly did not deserve shooting.

As we stepped off the bus, a rumble of thunder greeted us. Raindrops the size of ration coupons began bouncing off the pavement. I started to hurry back along the street.

"No!" Jeff called. "This way!" He was pointing up the street that was at right angles to the bus route.

"Don't be silly!" I shouted at him. "Kendall's back this way, three blocks, the driver said. C'mon!"

"No, listen! Up this street is shorter. If we go to Kendall, we have to walk back on Pine a half block in this direction, don't we? So if we go up this street to Pine and turn right, we …"

"All right, all right! Don't explain it to me, I'm drowning! Let's go."

This street ran through what seemed to be a factory. That blue industrial light flared eerily out into the night and turned the streaming rain into something living and writhing, not something sent from heaven that nurtures forget-me-nots and daisies. I was glad when we had done our two blocks on that thoroughfare and had swung right onto Pine; I wasn't in the mood to appreciate any theatrical effects, however delightfully macabre.

On Pine Street we hurried past a garage, a lumber yard, a junk yard, an abandoned used car lot. All were dark and deserted now and the city fathers of Hoboken weren't wasting any public utility on this neighborhood. The arcs of the infrequent street lights did not overlap; we had to walk through gray, shadowy patches that had me tightening my grip on Jeff's arm and glancing over my shoulder. I found myself scurrying from the haven of one comforting, if wan, lamp to the next, like a child playing a dangerous game.

"This should be our block now," Jeff said.

On the opposite side of the street rose the towering, unbroken wall of a huge warehouse. On this side there was a row of ramshackle frame houses of varying height. Some of them were boarded up, some of them had had their doors and windows gouged out, frames and all, and the rectangular holes stared at us like empty eyes. These were houses that were dead. Others still showed signs of life, a flicker of light at a window, a swing on a sagging porch moving in the wind, an empty milk bottle standing before the door.

Jeff stopped. The row of houses had ended; a high board fence stretched the rest of the block to what was, if we weren't lost,

Kendall Street. We walked back a few steps to the nearest inhabited house. Jeff held a burning match up to the door and found the number. We moved along to the next house. This was number 479; this was Laura Nichols' address. Jeff knocked on the door.

We waited only a moment.

The door creaked open. The fattest woman I had ever seen in my life stood looking at us. In her hand was an oil lamp with a smoked-black chimney. She looked at Jeff, then at me, then back at Jeff.

He said, "We've come to see Laura Nichols."

She held the lamp higher. Her dress under her arm was split clear to the middle of her enormous body. A dirty brown dog tried to squeeze past her and out. She put a foot down on the dog's back and pinioned it to the floor.

"Not out in the rain, Buddy," she said.

She had the sweetest, the most tinkling voice I had ever heard. It was a baby's voice. She lifted her foot and the dog ran back into the house. She laughed and the laugh matched her voice.

Jeff said again, "We've come to see Laura Nichols."

"Come in," the fat woman said, "come in."

"Thank you," Jeff said.

We went in.

CHAPTER NINE

THE door opened directly into a square room. There was a round dining table in the middle of it. Against one wall stood a single bed with a naked mattress upon it. Three doors, all closed, lined the rear of the room. Beneath the windows at the front were four cases of empty beer bottles. The fourth wall was taken up by a shining new upright piano.

The woman placed the lamp on top of the piano. She heaved herself over to one of the four straight chairs around the table and lowered herself into it. The chair disappeared completely. She picked up a quart paper carton, squinted into it and threw it over her shoulder. There was another carton on the table and she knocked it onto the floor with a flick of her hand.

Jeff and I were standing by the still open door. She smiled at us and said, "Shut the door and sit down until it stops raining. Harley should be back any time now with some more beer. What was that name you asked me about? Laura? Laura somebody?"

"Laura Nichols," Jeff said. He went to the table and sat opposite the woman. I took the chair at his side.

"Laura Nichols," the woman repeated. "Laura Nichols. Now, you know, that name's familiar. Wait till Harley gets here. Harley knows everybody, he'll be able to help you. You two married?"

"Yes," Jeff said.

"Well, then," she said to me, "take off your dress, darling. Hang it on the back of a chair, let it dry out."

"It isn't that wet," I said.

"Haven't you got a slip on under it? You needn't worry about Harley when he gets here. Harley never looks at another woman when I'm around. You know, there are days when I wish Harley and me were married. But when I mention it to him, he always says: 'What's the matter, Lettie, don't you trust me? Are you afraid,' he says, 'that I'll run away with a waitress?' She beamed and wagged her head happily. "That Harley! He says what he likes about me is my girlish figure!"

I looked at Jeff; he seemed to be interested only in what this woman was saying; he seemed to have forgotten about Laura Nichols. Then I saw that his eyes were studying each of the three closed doors across the rear wall.

"What's your name?" the woman was saying.

"They call me Jeff."

"Jeff, how much would you say I weighed?"

"How much would I say you weighed," Jeff repeated. He wasn't looking at the woman. His attention was centered upon the door at the left. "Well, let's see. You mean with all your clothes on?"

The woman chuckled; she slapped one knee, then the other. She acted as though she thought that was a good one. And she glanced over her shoulder to see what it was that intrigued Jeff.

But she said nothing about it.

"Two hundred pounds?" she asked. "Three hundred? Four hundred? Come on, Jeff, make a stab at it! Don't be bashful!"

"Two hundred and ninety," Jeff said. He stood up quickly. "I wonder if I could use your bathroom?"

"Why, of course! You're welcome to it!" She jerked a thumb at the door on the left. "Go right ahead. You better take the lamp; there isn't another light in the house."

"Thanks."

He took the lamp from the piano and walked around to the woman's side of the table. As he passed behind her he smiled at me, a smile that was supposed to dispel all my fears. It didn't.

"Two hundred and ninety," the woman chuckled. "That's pretty good. You only missed by eighty pounds. I'm three seventy. Maybe a little more." Her chuckle rose to a giggle. "I've been lax about my diet lately!"

Jeff opened the door. It swung in. He hesitated a moment, then went through it, closing it after him. Now the woman and I were sitting in total darkness. I heard her chair squeak.

"Have you lived here long?" I asked quickly. I wanted to hear her speak; I wanted to know where she was.

"All my life," she said. Her voice was where it had been; she hadn't moved. And my eyes, growing accustomed to the dark, verified that. I could make out a black blur across the table from me, the outline of her huge shoulders and tiny head. The chair squeaked again as she made herself more comfortable. "What's your name?" she asked.

"They call me Haila," I said. I tried to listen for Jeff. The stairs in this house must certainly be rickety and noisy, I should be able to hear his steps upon them. The woman kept me from hearing anything.

"Haila," she was saying. She said it several times. "That's an unusual name."

"I think so, too. My mother made a mistake."

"Oh, I like it!" She said it several more times. Jeff should be at the top of the stairs by now. He should be going into a room. It might not be the right room. It might take him a little while to find Laura. "My name is Lettie. I like that for a name, don't you?"

"Oh, yes!"

"Harley likes it, too."

She went on, but I wasn't listening to her. I was sure now that the door Jeff had gone through was slowly opening. A different kind of darkness inched wider and wider as it opened more. Now a small spot of gray moved up and down. Now it was jerking horizontally, it seemed to be pointing toward the … I got it. Jeff was signaling me with his handkerchief. He had hit a dead end; he wanted to get through one of the other doors and he needed my help. My help would be to cover his attempt, to screen any noise he might make.

The woman was saying, "Don't you think so, Haila?" She said it as though she had said it before.

"Oh, yes, Lettie!" I said. "I do think so! Excuse me, I was wondering about something. I mean, a funny thing happened to me today. …" I let my voice crescendo until it filled the room. I could see Jeff as he slipped along the wall, getting closer to the center door. I rattled on. "You telling me to take my dress off reminded me of it. I was shopping today and there was this salesgirl, you know what those girls have to go through, especially in this hot weather and this store wasn't air-conditioned …"

The woman interrupted me. "Jeff?" she said. Her chair squealed as she turned to look behind her.

"Yes," Jeff said. "That damn lamp went out. Do you have any matches, Haila?"

"Bring the lamp here," Lettie said. "I'll light it. I keep telling Harley we should have another lamp. Set it down here on the table."

There was a scratch and the woman had lit a kitchen match. Jeff held the lamp before her and lifted off the chimney, protecting his hand with his handkerchief.

"Sorry," he said.

"Don't be. That Harley! He won't buy me another lamp, but he goes and buys me a piano! A piano! Just because I happen to say that I wish I could play one. He brings home a piano on his truck and says, 'Here, Lettie, it's for you. Now you can learn to play.'

Just like that! And he won't even let me thank him!"

The lamp had flared up brightly now and I could see the reason for Jeff being stymied. The bathroom was not upstairs. Through the open door in the left corner I could see the gleam of enamel. A closet had probably been converted into a bath.

"Here's Harley!" the woman cried.

A man came stamping in out of the rain. He kicked shut the door behind him; his arms were filled with large brown paper bags. He, too, might have weighed three hundred and seventy pounds, but not because he was fat. He was a giant of a man; the floor shook under his tread. His face was boyish, pleasant. His hair was blond and curly. He looked at Jeff and me, a smiling question in his eyes.

"This is Jeff and Haila," Lettie said. "They're looking for somebody or other and I made them come in out of the rain."

"I'm glad," Harley said, "I'm glad you did. There's more than enough beer and stuff here. Sit down, folks, sit down!" He plopped the packages on the table. He pulled a quart container out of one and handed it to the woman. She lifted the cap and took a long drink.

Jeff said, "We're looking for Laura Nichols."

"Yes," said Lettie, "that was the name. Harley, tell them what it is you like about me!"

"I like Lettie," Harley said, "for her girlish figure."

"Didn't I tell you!" Lettie squealed. "Didn't I?"

"Jeff and Haila," Harley said, "did you ever see anything like Lettie? She's getting fatter every day."

"Stop it now, Harley!" Lettie gasped in delight. "Stop it now!"

"Who did you say you were looking for?" Harley asked.

"Laura Nichols."

"That name's familiar, isn't it, Harley?" Lettie asked.

"I never heard it," Harley said.

"I thought it sounded familiar."

"I never heard it, Lettie. And I know everyone in this neighborhood. Jeff, here's your quart of beer."

"No, thanks," Jeff said.

"Oh, you've got to have some beer or Lettie and me will think you don't like us. Here."

"Thanks," Jeff said.

"And here's yours, Haila. Drink up and you'll get nice and fat like Lettie."

"Thanks," I said.

"We have reason to believe," Jeff said, "that Laura Nichols is … is staying in this house."

"Here?" Harley asked. "In this house?" He was pulling things out of the other bags now, naming them as he did. "Rye bread. Liverwurst. Pickles. Where's the salami? Lettie loves salami. Jeff, only me and Lettie live here. Where did you get the idea this Laura lives here?"

"Look," Jeff said. "Let's stop having a party. Laura's father was here this morning and …"

"This morning?" Harley said. "Lettie, was anybody here this morning?"

"Not a soul."

"Not a soul was here this morning, Jeff," Harley said.

Jeff put his carton of beer on top of the piano. "I'm not going to leave here without that girl. I'm taking her back to her father. Where is she?"

Harley looked at Lettie; she shrugged. Harley looked back at Jeff and he shrugged. "I don't know what this is all about."

Jeff said, "If I tried to go upstairs, would you try to stop me?"

The man and the woman both rollicked with laughter. Lettie screamed, "If you tried to go upstairs would Harley try to stop you! That's a good one!"

"Go on upstairs, Jeff," Harley said. "Go on." He pulled a large flashlight from his hip pocket and snapped it on. He handed it to Jeff. "Is everything neat and tidy upstairs, Lettie?"

Lettie giggled. "I spent the whole afternoon cleaning up there!"

"Lettie, you work too hard! Haila, you want to come with us? You can tell me how good Lettie cleans. Jeff, we're ready if you are."

Jeff opened the door on the right. His flash bounced off the back wall of a closet. There was a coat or two on it, a pair of greasy overalls, a tattered umbrella, a pair of ice tongs, a pile of old newspapers and rows of empty beer bottles. Jeff closed the closet.

Harley pointed to the far corner. "That's the bathroom."

"I know," Jeff said.

The middle door swung into a narrow hallway. There was a door on each side of the center of it; it was open at the far end. Jeff started down the corridor. Harley followed him. I followed Harley.

First Jeff tried the door on the left. It was a bedroom and there was no one in it. Across the hall was a room half filled with neatly-cut, evenly piled fireplace logs. There were four worn truck tires and a heap of burlap bags. Jeff led the way to the end of the hall and into a kitchen that stretched the width of the house. There were two doors in it. One opened onto a back yard. The other was a closet.

"How," Jeff asked, "do you get upstairs?"

"Follow me," Harley said, "unless you don't want to get wet."

He took the flashlight and ducked out into the back yard, Jeff and I at his heels. We followed him to the middle of the yard where he turned around, facing the house. He was chuckling as he played the light on the wall of the house. Slowly he raised the gleaming circle, spraying the windows of the kitchen, then lifting it higher. I heard Jeff's gasp of amazed disbelief.

The light had swept across two feet of clapboard above the windows, flicked over the eaves of a sloping tin roof, then coned out through a curtain of rain and darkness. The house at 479 Pine Street, Hoboken, was a one-story house.

Harley's chuckle had exploded into a roar of laughter. He dashed into the kitchen leaving Jeff and me standing there in the rain. It was a moment before I realized that we were being drenched. I took Jeff by the arm.

"Let's get out of the ..."

"There's no second floor," Jeff said. "Nichols told us that he went up to the second floor."

"Jeff, let's go in."

We had to grope our way back into the kitchen, down the hall-way to the front room. Harley had joined Lettie; we could hear his joyful guffaws and her soprano squeals as they rejoiced in the success of their joke on us. Jeff waited until they had exhausted themselves and had turned to their beer for revival.

He said, "And you don't have a telephone."

"What's that?" Harley asked, grinning.

"This man … Nichols … he asked me to help him. He said his daughter was being held in this house. He said he talked to her on the phone here this morning. …"

The man and woman went off into another fit of glee. Harley shouted, "Lettie, tomorrow remind me to get a second floor and a telephone!"

"This man Nichols," Lettic said to us, "he's a card!"

"Is he a friend of yours?" Harley asked. "Does he often play jokes like this?"

"We never saw him before," Jeff said, talking more to himself than the others. "Why should he want us to come over here to Hoboken? Or why did he want to get us out of New York? And who is he and why …"

"Jeff!" I said. "If he wanted to get us out of New York … Jeff, maybe something's happened to Diane!"

He shook his head. "We weren't bodyguarding Diane. She wouldn't let us. We couldn't have stopped anything from happening to her but … but we'd better get back."

Harley stood up. He drained the quart carton of beer and slapped it down on the table. "I got the truck outside. I'll take you to the ferry."

"That would be fine," Jeff said, "but we hate to …"

"The least Harley can do," Lettie said, "after the fun we had tonight! You'll come again?"

"Sure they will," Harley said. "And you'll cook for them, Lettie, and they'll come back once a week as long as they live!"

"Harley," Lettie said, "find out in the truck what this is all about. Maybe you can help Jeff and Haila."

"All right, I will. I'll bring back some more beer, Lettie. Be good, now. Are you two ready?"

We said we were and, after a few minutes of apologies and thanks, we left Lettie and went out to the truck. Harley held the light and we climbed into the cab. On the side of the cab door in proud letters was painted: Harley Olsen, Ice, Coal, Wood. We started for the ferry.

As we rode through Hoboken Jeff told the story of Austin Marshall's murder, of Robert Nichols' appearance, of his fantastic story. He promised, at Harley's request, that we would come back and tell him the solution of these mysteries if they were ever solved.

Our conversation dwindled to a halt as Jeff went into a mental tussle with the solution of said mysteries. Harley leaned over the steering wheel as he peered through the rainswept windshield. He was humming a song. A song I knew but couldn't place. I was about to ask him what it was when Jeff spoke.

"Hey, that's a Dartmouth song!"

"That's right," Harley said. "I got a brother at Dartmouth, he teaches chemistry."

"Frederick Olsen!" Jeff exclaimed. "He's your brother?"

"Yeah, but I don't like him much."

"I don't, either," Jeff said. "I flunked chemistry."

Harley saw me looking at him and he laughed. "Haila, I came over here to drink some beer one night in nineteen twenty-seven, and I stayed. I like it. I like it fine. While there's still beer in Hoboken, I'm staying. And then, there's Lettie. Well, folks, this is the ferry and you're going to have to run to make the boat. So long!"

"So long and thanks a lot! We owe you and Lettie …"

"Write us a letter! You know our address!"

Harley's laugh chased us into the station. We slipped under the descending gates, climbed to the upstairs cabin, and sat down. I was tired; too tired to even think about Robert Nichols and what he had done to us. I let Jeff take care of that. I just sat, waiting to get home.

And at long, long last we did. The apple-pie tidiness of our house gave proof that Chuckie's mother had been there that afternoon and done her daily duty. All the disorder that last night's prowler had left behind him had been removed. The furniture glowed with Mrs. Clancy's fervid polishing; ashtrays and lamp bases and woodwork sparkled from her scrubbing. Her daily report, typed à la one finger at my request because of her impossible handwriting, was in its usual place in Jeff's portable. Today it was slightly repetitious. Mr. Tony Gilbert, it said, telephoned at four. Mr. Gilbert called at four-fifteen. At four-thirty a call ... Mr. G. "Never no message," was the finale.

"Tony must have heard of our visit to Mrs. Davisson," Jeff said. "Well, I guess he'll call again."

While Jeff mixed us a couple of anti-chill drinks, I changed into an old skirt and older sweater. My drink was waiting for me on the coffee table in the living room. Jeff was not waiting for me; his drink was half gone.

He shook his head and said, "Lord, I feel silly!"

"Jeff, I wish you'd call Diane. I'm worried about her."

"All right."

The Phillips' butler, I gathered from Jeff's conversation, informed him that the lady of the house was not in, that she had gone out immediately after dinner, that her destination was unknown. Jeff hung up.

"Well," he said, "as of dinner she was still in good health. Stop fretting about her, Haila."

"Nichols might have been following her. When he heard in the bar that you were helping her ... oh, yes, I know you weren't guarding her. But how could he know that?"

"Your theory's as good as any I've got. In fact, I haven't got any." He finished the rest of his drink.

"Do you think we'll ever see or hear from Nichols again?"

"No. Do you, Haila?"

"No. Not unless he thinks he's big enough to keep me from socking him one on the nose."

Jeff smiled. "That story of his! Were we taken in! We had tears in our eyes ... poor Laura!"

"Why, why, why did he do that to us?"

"It's connected in some way with Marshall's murder ... but how, how, how? Pardon me while I go raving mad."

"Jeff, there's one little thing. Nichols picked an actual street number to send us to. That means he ..."

"That means he knows something about Hoboken, that's all that means. You telephone all the people in the world who know that there's a Pine Street in Hoboken while I finish your drink."

"Stay away from my drink! It's saving my life."

Jeff got up and roamed the room. "I wish I'd listened to myself when I told Hankins this case wasn't going to be solved. I haven't got one thing to work on, not one thing! If I wanted to work on the case tonight, what would I do?"

"I guess you know that's a rhetorical question."

He flung himself back down on the loveseat. "The hell with murder, Robert Nichols and so forth. I'm going to curl up with a good book. Have we got a good book?"

"Let's talk, Jeff, let's have a quiet evening at home just sitting and talking. You know, like a married couple."

"All right. Did you have a nice day, darling?"

"Yes. Were you busy at the office?"

"Things were slack today."

"Is this the slack season?"

"No, it isn't really. But today was slack."

"Just one of those slack days, hum, dear?"

"Um-hum. Saw Charley today."

"Charley Brewster?"

"Charley Munn."

"How's Charley?"

"Charley Munn?"

"Brewster."

"He can't kick. Ho-hum, but I'm tired tonight. I think I'll turn in. I've had a very slack day."

"Me, too. You empty the ashtrays, I'll turn down the beds."

"Boy, am I going to hit that hay!"

"Me, too. Will I pound that pillow!"

The telephone and the door bells rang simultaneously.

CHAPTER TEN

Jeff went to the door; I answered the phone.

"Well, well," a voice said, "so you finally got home!"

"Who is it?" I asked.

"Diane. The Beekman Place hag, remember?"

"Diane! Are you … are you all right?"

"What do you mean?" The lightness sagged out of the voice. "You sound as if you didn't expect me to be all right."

"No, I just meant … I was being polite. Forgive me."

"Haila, I want to see Jeff again. Right away, may I? I'm around the corner in a drugstore. I've been calling you since dinner. It's important."

"We'll be here, Diane."

"Thanks. It'll take me three minutes to get there. Good-bye." She hung up and I hung up.

Tony Gilbert walked into the living room ahead of Jeff. He was handling his cane tonight, not as a decoration, but as if he really needed it. His game leg was apparently one of those allergic to weather. But the rest of him was in fine form. His smile and gallant bow made me feel like the ingenue in a Schubert operetta.

"Haila," he said, "I hope I'm intruding."

"Hello, Tony. Have a chair. And a drink."

"No, thanks, no drink." He sat on the arm of a loveseat. "I can only stay a second."

"Who called, Haila?" Jeff asked.

"Diane. She's coming to see us. In three minutes … two by now."

"Diane Phillips is coming here?" Tony slid off the arm and into the seat of his chair. "That's fine! There is a beautiful woman! Not for Tony, but beautiful. Why is Diane coming here? I hope it's none of my business."

"Don't be silly," Jeff said. "Diane and Haila are trading recipes."

Tony grinned. "It's none of my business. Jeff, are you and Haila going to trade recipes with the cops? And you know what I mean! How do you like Marjorie Davisson? I don't blame you for following her. But if the cops start following her, I'm going to blame you."

"Don't worry," Jeff said.

Tony leaned forward. "Look. If it becomes an item that Tony and Marjorie are thataway, Mr. Davisson is going to be irate. And if Mr. Davisson becomes irate, he'll lock Marjorie in her room. And I'll become irate."

"We won't breathe a word," Jeff said. "But not because of you, pal. Because of Mrs. Davisson and her husband. We don't want the Marriage Doctor's radio audience to be disillusioned."

"Troys," Tony said, "you're worthy people. You deserve tickets to my show. I'll attend to that immediately."

"That's bribery," Jeff said.

"Without a doubt."

"Make them orchestra seats," Jeff said. "In the center."

The doorbell rang. While Jeff attended to it, Tony composed a conversational lyric to the glory that was Marjorie Davisson's. If he went on like this to Marjorie herself, and there was no reason to think he didn't, there was little question why she risked her husband's ire to see Tony Gilbert. He was more than a lover; he was a fan club.

Jeff ushered Diane into the living room. Rain glistened on her white face, dripped off the brim of her hat. Her eyes were clouded with anxiety, her mouth set in a hard line. That was until she saw Tony. Then, instantly, her face did one of its remarkable quick-changes. It became the indolent, sulky mask of a bored woman; Diane's camouflage. Her voice was lazy and uninterested in itself when she turned back to Jeff and spoke.

"You should have warned me! If I'd known Tony Gilbert was

here, I'd have worn my glamour!"

The actor grinned maliciously. "Beautiful, sarcastic Mrs. Phillips! I adore her! I could strangle her!"

"Dear Tony! Why aren't you at work, darling? Oh, no, you don't play tonight, do you?"

"No, sweet. Two performances on the Sabbath. No performance on Monday. Do you mind?"

"Tony, darling, this being your only free night, why don't you do something? Go … bowling or something. Wouldn't that be fun?"

"So sorry, adorable, don't bowl. My leg, you know." He tapped it with his cane. "Furthermore, I like it here. With you."

"A charming character!" Diane turned to me. "Tony's such a charming character. Did you know? He burns down old ladies' homes."

"Young ladies' homes," Tony said.

"Darling, aren't you stupid to work at the canteens? I thought the FBI had all the workers fingerprinted as an espionage precaution. Aren't you afraid your criminal past will catch up with you, the least of which is arson?"

"Mrs. Phillips," Tony laughed, "how you do run on!"

Diane seated herself with studied languidness and lit a cigarette. She and Tony sent each other frozen smiles. She was determined to wait him out, and he taunted her by elaborately making himself more comfortable on the love seat. Jeff was enjoying their duel, but the lengthening pause was beginning to get on my nerves. I cleared my throat and made a feeble pass at some conversation.

"Tony," I said brightly, "you and Chuckie's mother had quite a session this afternoon, didn't you?"

He shifted his eyes to me. "Chuckie's mother? I'm afraid I don't …"

"Mrs. Clancy. My cleaning lady; Jeff's secretary." I pointed to the tabulation of Tony's calls, still rolled in the typewriter.

"Oh, yes!" Tony sauntered over to the desk and glanced at the list. He chuckled. "She missed one. Mr. Gilbert also called at five." He took a step toward the door. "Well," he said, "I'm afraid I must be …" He stopped; he had caught the pleased relief on

Diane's face. He went back to the loveseat and sat down again. "All right. If everyone insists, I'll stay. But only for an hour or two. And then I must run."

"Tony," Diane said.

"Yes, Mrs. Phillips?"

"Tony, darling." Her voice was slow and overemphatic. "Are you planning to produce another play?"

The question wiped the smile from his face. His eyes went on guard and he stared evenly at Diane; he didn't speak.

"Haila," Diane said, "did you know that once Tony Gilbert was going to produce a play on Broadway? A vehicle for himself, a starring vehicle? Did you know that, Jeff?"

"No," Jeff said.

"Oh, yes, yes, indeed! It seems that ..."

"Diane," Tony said carefully, "you're boring the Troys. The Troys aren't interested. They're bored. Talk about something else, Diane."

"Dear Tony is so modest," Diane said. "Darling, I'm certain that the Troys won't let this go any further. For instance, if the janitor walked in now, or if that policeman friend of theirs named Hankins happened by, they wouldn't tell him. I mean ... why should they?" She swung her head toward us, but her eyes remained on Tony. "It seems that Tony had found a play with a part in it worthy of his talents and he had raised the money to produce it ... everything was all set. But then something happened. The play was never produced. Tony, just what *did* happen to ... Oh, are you leaving, darling? Must you rush?"

The actor had risen. He regarded Diane with a cold, murderous distaste that pulled her to her feet. They stood facing each other. If they had been animals, they would have been at each other's throat.

Jeff said, "Haila, is there any fudge in the house? I feel in the mood for fudge."

Tony relaxed; he smiled. He flipped his malacca stick under his arm. He was jaunty. Holding a hand out to Diane, he said, "Mrs. Phillips, I'm sure you and the Troys have so much to talk about ... good night now, it's been lovely."

"Good night, Tony, darling, and hasn't it been lovely?" She took his outstretched hand. "Good night."

"And Mrs. Phillips, don't be a gossip." He tightened his grip on her hand. She winced and tried to withdraw it. "Don't be a gossip, Mrs. Phillips, don't."

"You're hurting me, Tony!"

"Oh, so sorry! Tony plays too rough!" He kissed her hand and let it slide from his. "Give my love to Mr. Phillips, Mrs. Phillips. So long, Troys."

Jeff followed him out of the room.

Diane watched them go before she slumped into a chair. She brushed her fingers across her forehead in a tired, indecisive gesture, and the brilliant scarlet of her nails looked giddy and incongruous against her white, drawn face.

I edged over to the French windows and looked out into the dark little two-by-four garden. Just visible was the cement boy holding the cement fish; our non-founting fountain. Around it was Jeff's fruitless attempt at big-city agriculture, a triple row of sweet corn that had been knee high all right on the Fourth of July, but had still been knee high on the Fourth of September. Over in a corner under the sumac tree were the two deck chairs where Jeff used to insist I sit with him and watch the corn sway in the breeze. That was all long ago, years ago. In fact, it was before we had taken Chuckie Clancy to Central Park to sail his boat; it was the day before yesterday. Time, it seemed, didn't necessarily fly. There were exceptions to that rule.

Before Jeff could cross the room to the cigarette he had left burning in the ashtray on the desk, Diane was flooding him with words. She had come alive again, vital, urgent.

"Why," she asked, "was Tony here? What did he want?"

"I have no idea," Jeff said inaccurately.

"But it wasn't a social call, was it? You didn't know him before … before Austin's death?"

"No, we didn't."

"Then he came to see you about the murder! What did he tell you? Does he know something?"

"If he does, it's still a secret from me."

"Did he come to talk about me?" She pressed on. "Did he tell you anything about me?"

"No, Diane."

"Just now ... when you went with him to the door ... he didn't say anything?"

"No," Jeff laughed. "We discussed the weather."

She looked at him sharply with ill-concealed suspicion, but she gave up her third-degree. She said quietly, "I've often wondered if he'd guessed about me. About Austin and me. He's such a prying person, he lives on scandal. It would be like him to set the police against William by showing them that he had a motive for Austin's murder. That would be very like Tony. That would amuse him ..." She let the words trail off into space. She sat staring at nothing. Jeff's chuckle snapped her eyes back to him. "What are you laughing at?"

"I think you and Tony have each other under control. You know something about him; he knows something about you. Sort of two-way blackmail. Neither of you will talk any more about each other, will you?"

"Jeff, that was a silly business, that between Tony and me just now."

"If you told me about Tony and the play he didn't produce it might help me to solve the murder. Remember, you paid me a thousand dollars to solve it. You'd be protecting your investment."

"Tony and the play have nothing to do with the murder!" She leaned toward Jeff in her eagerness to convince him. "Forget about that, please. It was silly and unfair of me. ... I only did it because Tony made me so angry. He was only staying here because he knew I wanted him to go."

"All right, Diane."

She extracted a cigarette from her slim silver case and looked helplessly around for a match. Jeff lit the cigarette and sat beside her. He said, "Did you ever hear of a man named Robert Nichols?"

"Robert Nichols? No, I don't think so. Why?"

"I'm looking for him. He owes me taxi fare. Diane, do you remember that little man who was listening to us in the Third Avenue dive this afternoon?"

"Yes, I do. He had on a brand-new hat."

"Right," Jeff said. "Did you ever see him before?"

"No, I don't think so."

"He didn't look familiar?"

"No. Who is he, Jeff?"

"He's Robert Nichols. Or at least he was this afternoon. And he owes me a taxi ride. We shared a cab. And he left me with the check."

"Something has happened," Diane said, "and you're not telling me. Is it because you don't want me to worry? Jeff, I can't be any more frightened than I am now! I can't stand it much longer! That feeling of being watched, of being followed and spied upon! Not knowing who is doing it nor why it's being done! Jeff, you've got to find the murderer!"

"It isn't that I don't want to, Diane. Believe me."

"If you don't hurry the police will stumble on William's motive … they'll find out about Austin and me. They'll indict William for the murder … and they mustn't do that, they mustn't!" Suddenly she went limp. When she spoke again her voice was dreary and emotionless. "Another thing. William knows that I've been having something to do with you, something that I've been hiding from him. He knows that I met you in that bar this afternoon."

"How did he find out?"

She shrugged dismally. "He must have followed you and Haila and watched from outside. He hasn't told me that yet. He's only shown me that he knows I'm doing something and that he disapproves of it, whatever it is." She twisted around to face Jeff squarely, her hands clenched under her chin. "I can't take much more, I can't! I'm trying to help William! I'm trying to save him from the police! And yet he suspects me of … of … Oh, I don't mind doing this, I don't mind the danger I'm in, or the risks I'm taking, but when William …"

The jangle of the telephone snuffed out her hysteria. I slipped quietly to the desk and answered it. A nasal female voice that I had never heard before asked to speak, please, with Mrs. William Phillips. I covered the mouthpiece with the palm of my hand and said, "Diane. For you."

Her gaze wandered vaguely in my direction, her eyes not focusing upon me. "For … me?" she muttered. "But who could possibly know that I'm here?"

She crossed to the desk and picked up the phone tentatively, cautiously, as if at any moment it might explode in her face. There were tiny creases of bewilderment lining her brow as she raised the instrument to her ear.

"Yes?" she said. "This is Diane Phillips."

A moment … and then an expression of horrified disbelief swept away the frown. Her hand on the telephone tautened until the knuckles showed white through the paleness of her skin. She opened her mouth and her lips formed an affirmative that never became an audible sound. I could hear the voice that came through the wires, crackling and sputtering in a rapid torrent of speech, but no single word of it was distinguishable. Abruptly, the voice halted.

Diane said carefully, "Yes. Yes, I understand."

She replaced the phone in its cradle. Then she swooped it up again and looked at it thoughtfully. Her index finger moved toward the dial. But, almost as suddenly, she changed her mind. She slammed the phone back with a decisive bang and turned to us.

"I must go … immediately."

"May we help, Diane?" Jeff asked.

For a long quiet minute she eyed Jeff, then she answered in a muffled tone. "No," she said, "you … can't help me." She snatched up her coat and slipped into it. She slung the strap of her big handbag over her shoulder, crumpled her gloves into a ball and thrust them into a pocket. At the doorway she stopped and turned back. Almost inaudibly, she said, "Thank you. But, no. No, I can't ask you to help."

Then she was gone.

Jeff was pulling raincoats out of the closet before the running click of Diane's heels had faded from the outside hall. He tossed me mine; he shoved himself into his.

"Hurry," he said.

"We're going to follow her?" I asked unnecessarily.

"On second thought, *I* am going to follow her."

"Then I'll follow you."

"Okay," Jeff said. "Okay."

A chilling gush of wind and rain met us at the front door; even the weather was trying to come in out of this dismal night. At the Waverly Place corner of crooked little Gay Street stood Diane, one hand clutching her coat collar tight against the downpour, the other waving wildly as she futilely beckoned a passing cab. She turned suddenly and looked back at our house. Jeff and I retreated rapidly into the vestibule. But if Diane had spotted us in that one brief glance, she gave no indication of it. She turned back to the street at once and returned to her efforts of flagging down a taxi.

"Wait here," Jeff said. "And don't take your eyes off the lady."

He disappeared around the angle of Gay Street, heading for its Christopher Street end. I stood there, watching Diane, hoping that Jeff would get a cab at least as soon as she did. The Troy luck paid off; Diane's cab had just flicked out of sight when another pulled to a halt in front of me. Jeff held open the door and I jumped in beside him.

"Where is she?" he said.

"Just turned the corner a second ago. She's headed for Sixth Avenue."

Jeff leaned forward to give instructions to the driver. I rubbed a peephole onto the fogged window, bringing into my line of vision the doorway of the house next to ours. A dark figure was huddled in its darker shadows. I wiped the window with a sweep of my arm and pressed my face against it, straining to see better. The figure, only a blurred and distorted outline through the rain and gloom, quickly withdrew from sight.

I grabbed Jeff's arm. "Look!" I said. "In that doorway there ... someone's hiding ..."

Our cab lurched forward as Jeff turned to look, but he didn't ask the driver to stop. "Probably someone who ducked in out of the wet," he said.

I twisted in the seat and made myself another peephole in the rear window. Just as we turned into Waverly Place, I caught a glimpse of a figure as it darted out of that doorway. I thought I saw it make a quick move as if to run after our cab. But I wasn't certain, not certain enough to report my suspicion to Jeff.

Diane's taxi, having been held up by the traffic light at the corner, was swinging into Sixth Avenue now and heading north. It picked up speed and so did we, staying fifty yards behind it. Jeff was hunched forward, his attention glued in that direction. But I found myself unable to concentrate on the pursuit of Diane Phillips; I kept turning to peer out the back window, searching for a running figure in the dimness of the night.

By the time we had reached Thirty-fourth Street, I realized that there was no way of knowing for sure whether Jeff and I, as we followed Diane, were also being followed. On this storm-struck evening every cab in New York City was in motion; a parade of them was moving up Sixth Avenue. It was impossible to tell if one of those behind us was being used by my friend, the shadow. I wrenched that uncomfortable feeling out of my mind and forced myself to keep my eyes straight ahead.

Diane's driver led us off Sixth Avenue and over to Fifth where our chase picked up momentum. We moved rapidly through the dimmed-out Forties and Fifties and into the practically blacked-out Sixties. To our right stood the line of tall apartment houses, their lighted windows curtained against the dreariness of the night. To our left lay Central Park, bleak now and foreboding. Tonight Manhattan's garden spot was hardly looking its verdant best.

At Seventy-second Street, Diane's cab swung into a wide U-turn and halted on the park side of the Avenue. We slowed to a crawl while the traffic light clicked to yellow and then to red and gave us a legitimate excuse to stop and spy on Diane. She was standing on the sidewalk now. Her cab pulled away from the curb and joined the procession that was moving down the Avenue, but still she stood there, a lonely, desolate figure in the rain. I was about to suggest to Jeff that she must be waiting for someone, when she wheeled around and disappeared into the park entrance.

Jeff was looking at me strangely.

"What's wrong?" I asked.

"You shuddered, sweetheart."

"I don't blame myself for shuddering. She must be going back to ... to that bench on the knoll. ..."

"Go home, Haila. I'll take care of her."

"And who'll take care of you? Let's go."

We got out of our cab and dodged our way through the traffic to the park side of the street. We went into the entrance and walked along the path to the lake. The wind had whipped up a miniature storm-at-sea on the pool and, as we skirted it, the slapping of water on concrete sounded like a warning. Through the almost pitch darkness we moved on, our caution increasing with every step. At last we stood at the foot of the little knoll. Before us a flight of long-treaded steps rose to the bench where Austin Marshall had met his death.

Diane was nowhere to be seen.

CHAPTER ELEVEN

WHEN Jeff raised his foot onto the first step, I reached out and put a hand on his arm. He turned back to me.

"Haila," he whispered, "did you hear something?"

"No, I didn't. ..."

"What's wrong then?"

"Do we have to go up there, Jeff? I mean ... I don't think Diane's up there. Why would she go up there?"

"Haila." He put his arm around my shoulders. "I don't blame you. That isn't a nice place. You wait for me down here."

"All right," I said. Then I said, "By myself?"

"Well ..."

"Go slowly, I can't see. And take my hand."

"Don't be frightened, Haila."

"Who's frightened?"

"You are."

"That's right. Aren't you frightened, Jeff?"

"Of what?"

"If I knew what to be frightened of, I wouldn't be so frightened. It's this not knowing."

"We'll soon know," Jeff said.

"Shhh!"

"What did you hear?"

"You. On second thought, I don't mind not knowing."

"Haila, you're hurting my hand! C'mon, let's go."

There was no one, no one that we could see on top of the hill. There was no movement but the uneasy stirring of the shrubbery in the wind and no sound but the drumming of the rain on the pocket-sized plateau. We stood there waiting in the darkness … waiting and listening.

Things began to pile up, mount and crescendo toward a climax that didn't come. I found myself listening for a bloodcurdling scream or a ghastly, mirthless chuckle. Or, at least, the rattle of a chain. But nothing happened … just the rain and the wind and the darkness … nothing else.

"Jeff," I whispered, "she isn't here."

"Wait a second."

He fished his pencil flashlight from his pocket. Its beam swept across the empty bench, along the edge of the thirty-foot cliff that was one side of the knoll, toward the rock-strewn slope that was the other side.

The snapping sound we heard came from behind us, a sound not made by the wind or the rain. Jeff swung the light around to meet it. Frozen flat against a tree trunk stood Diane. The light was not strong enough to outline her sharply, but it was enough to pick up her white-gloved hand as it darted wildly out, to catch the brief flash of bright metal that flew out of the hand.

Jeff dropped the beam to the ground between Diane and us, and it washed the little graveled path we stood on. It caught the small bright object still rolling on the walk. Jeff bent over and picked it up. It was a gold elephant, less than an inch in height, perfectly carved. Three tiny links of chain, the end one twisted out of shape, hung from its back. Jeff stepped toward Diane and extended the jeweled elephant to her. She made no move to take it; she stood trembling and silent. Jeff withdrew his hand.

"Diane," he said, "are you all right?"

She nodded, her wide, frightened gaze held on Jeff's face.

"Why did you come here, Diane? What is all this? That phone call … did someone ask you to meet him here?"

"No … they told me …"

"Who was it?" Jeff interrupted.

"I don't know. It was a woman, I'd never heard her voice before, she didn't tell me her name. She said that there was something here, near the bench where Austin Marshall had been murdered, that would interest me. Something, she said, that the police had overlooked in their search. I don't know what she could have meant. There's nothing here, nothing. I've looked …"

Jeff held out his hand again and played the light on the gold trinket. "She couldn't have meant that, could she, Diane?" She stared at him without answering, as if she hadn't heard his question. "Why did you throw it away, Diane?"

"Throw it away …" She repeated his words dully. Then, suddenly, she came back to life with a start. "Throw it away! I didn't! I dropped it. Your flashlight startled me and I … I dropped it!"

"Whose is it?"

"Mine! It's mine! My husband gave it to me. He used to wear it on his watch chain. …"

Jeff said, "It looks as if it had been torn off your husband's watch chain."

"He tore it off to give it to me. That was the only way he could get it off. But what does it matter that …"

"When did he give it to you, Diane?"

"Long ago. Weeks ago! He hasn't worn it for weeks, he hasn't had it!" Her voice rose and the words rang out in desperation. "I didn't find this here, I tell you! I brought it here with me, I dropped it! I've been wearing it, not William! You can't make me say that William … Stop it! Please, stop it!"

With a choking sound she broke past us and fled down the hill. I could still hear her stumbling down the steps, still hear her muffled sobbing when it happened. I felt the brush of something as it zinged past my ear and, at the same time, heard the crack of the shot as it was fired. Jeff kicked my feet from under me. I hit the mud and went into a skid. My feet bumped into a rock as the second bullet whizzed by.

Somewhere close to me Jeff was yelling.

"Diane!" he shouted. "Diane, duck!"

I could hear him racing down the stepped hill, shouting at the top of his lungs. I scrambled to my feet ... this was no place for me to be left alone. But the sound of a third shot sent me sprawling in the mud again in self defense. I stayed where I was. Jeff's footsteps splashed on, grew fainter in the distance, and were gone. Then there was quiet; no more shots, no more shouts, no more footsteps.

I waited, crouching low, until my nerves and the muddy wetness that soaked through my clothes wouldn't permit me to remain immobile a second longer. I lifted my head cautiously and looked around. I saw nothing but thick, dripping shrubbery. I got to my knees and looked for the lake. I couldn't locate it. I searched for the shrouded lights of Fifth Avenue and they were out of sight. Now, alone and lost, this once charming hillock seemed even darker and direr than it had before.

Carefully, a little at a time, I rose to a standing position. The possibility that I might be mistaken for Diane by her murderous assailant was not remote enough to bring me the slightest comfort. I turned all the way around, seeking some landmark that would steer me out of the park, but all that I could see was shrubbery. Never in my life had I been so completely surrounded by shrubbery.

I started groping my way forward and an unfriendly branch stuck one of its twigs in my eye. That wouldn't happen again. Reversing myself, I began backing through the brambles. I was doing fine enough to momentarily forget my plight and wonder where Diane and Jeff and their gunman friend might be, when my left foot, in quest of a safe spot to step on, could find no spot whatsoever. I stretched it back further, lowered it to one side, swung it to the other. I couldn't touch a thing. It simply groped about in mid-air.

This is silly, I thought, this is absurd. There must be something ... and then, suddenly, it didn't seem silly at all. I knew where I was. I had backed my way to the edge of that precipitous cliff.

Frantically, I threw myself forward. My grounded foot slipped and for one awful second all of me was in midair. My hands touched cold, wet stone, slipped along its surface, miraculously found a crevice in the rock, and held there.

Holding tight, I moved my feet along the wall, trying to find another crevice in which to anchor them. There was none. I was dangling by my hands from the smooth face of a cliff. When my hands became too weak to hold my one hundred and twenty pounds any longer, my body would plummet down into the abyss below …

"Jeff!" I screamed. "Jeff!"

There was no answer.

I must conserve my strength, I must hold on and … or would be better to let go now? Let go and get it over with. Perhaps nothing more would happen than two broken legs … but I didn't want two broken legs. Hold on, Haila, hold on for dear life. I could feel my arms begin to pull out of their sockets. My fingers began to …

"Jeff!" I wailed. "Jeff!"

Again there was no answer.

My husband was busy saving somebody else's wife's life. He would come back to find my broken body crumpled at the foot of the cliff. Or maybe my body wouldn't be found for days … There was a movement behind me, directly behind me. Something was moving through the air, coming at me … but that couldn't be unless … No, vultures always waited until after …

A beam of light washed the wall, enveloping me in its brightness.

"Hello, Haila," Jeff said.

"Hello, hell! Get a ladder, Jeff! Call the fire department! Call …"

"Haila, darling." His voice was coming closer. "Look down, dear."

I looked down. The circle of light dropped and held. I could see my feet as they hung there, two scant inches above the ground. It was not the cliff I had been hanging from. It was a measly boulder, just tall enough for me to stretch full length upon. Jeff took me in his arms and kissed me; he was laughing.

"Take your hands off me!" I snapped at him. "Don't you touch me!"

I walked away from him, counting my broken fingernails. There were nine of them. Jeff came behind me, flashing the light on the ground.

"Haila," he said, "how long were you hanging there?"

"None of your business! I don't want your sympathy, thank you! I was very comfortable hanging there."

"You looked very cute, too, Haila. Except … I hate to tell you this …"

"Tell me what!"

"Your slip was showing."

"Oh, be quiet! Jeff! Diane … where is she? Did you find her?"

"No. She got away from me in the dark and so did the man with the gun. I hope she's on her way home. We'd better get the hell over there and see if she's all right. And stays all right."

The Phillips' manservant regarded our muddy and bedraggled clothes with a lofty distaste. His eyebrows shot up into two pointed arches and his voice droned through his long nose.

"Mrs. Phillips," he said, "has retired for the night."

At Jeff's flat demand for an immediate audience with his mistress, the distaste became horrified revulsion.

"Mrs. Phillips," he gasped, "is not to be disturbed under any circumstances!"

"We want to see her," Jeff insisted, "for her own good. You'd better …"

The door began to close, gently but very firmly, in our faces.

"Do you know who I am?" Jeff asked. The door continued to swing toward us. "I'm Humphrey Bogart." He kicked the door briskly and it burst out of the butler's hands and swung wide open. "I'm Jimmy Cagney," Jeff said, "before he started dancing." He pulled the man's coat down off his shoulders and buttoned it. He tilted his head toward me and said, "This is my moll, she's poison. If she kisses you, you'll die."

The man's hands flapped helplessly at his sides, his eyes and mouth gaped wide. Jeff took my arm and hustled me through the mirrored vestibule. We ran through the living room, up the broad, curving staircase to Diane's bedroom. There Jeff became the gentleman again; he knocked.

The door inched open noiselessly and the maid who had carried Diane's message to us that afternoon stuck her head out. When she recognized us she immediately slipped into the hall, pulling the door shut behind her. But I had had time to catch a glimpse of Diane as she lay in her big satin-upholstered bed. Her face was deathly white against the pale green linens, but her eyes had been closed and she seemed to be resting quietly and securely.

The maid said, "What is it? Has something happened?"

"Is Mrs. Phillips all right?"

The maid looked puzzled. "All right? Yes, she's all right. She came home just now with a chill and a headache. She got caught in the rain. But she'll be all right again in the morning. She ... What is it? Is something the matter?"

"Yes. Mrs. Phillips is in danger. Stay with her all night. Will you do that? Don't leave her for a single second."

The maid swallowed hard. "Is it ... is it something to do with the murder?"

"Yes, it's something to do with the murder."

A look of mingled comprehension and fear crossed the woman's face. She said softly, "I understand. I won't leave her, not at all. I'll ..."

A double set of footsteps were pounding up the stairs behind us. William Phillips, followed by his still purple-faced butler, appeared in the corridor. Seeing us, Phillips' expression of alarm changed to indignation. As if they had been robots, he curtly dismissed the two servants. But the maid, before she disappeared into the room, cabled Jeff a nod of understanding.

Phillips tapped his toe against the carpet. He looked like a seventeenth century New England schoolteacher about to take the rod to a pair of nefarious dunces. "Mr. and Mrs. Troy," he demanded, "what is the meaning of this?"

"Your wife was attacked again tonight. This time with a gun." In a modified form, Jeff told him what had happened. He omitted the fact that he had been employed by Diane and skirted the fact that we had followed her to Central Park. His story sounded as if we had met her, by accident, at the scene of the crime. Phillips listened to his spiel in a silence so polite and patient that it was obvious he wasn't accepting Jeff's every word as gospel truth.

"We'll discuss this further in my room," he said at last. "Follow me, please."

Phillips' bedroom was as coldly formal and uncompromising as the man who slept in it. Mahogany chests, bare and grim, stiff, severely simple curtains, dark brown leather chairs. The few pictures were of European cathedrals in black and white, and did nothing to relieve the starkness of the gray walls. The rug was a dun-colored broadloom. There was not a single personal article in sight; no clothes, no books or magazines, no ashtray or cigarettes on the bed table. The place looked ready for a military inspection by some Prussian martinet.

Phillips motioned us, not too graciously, to the leather chairs. He himself stood, pompous and formal, in front of a closed-up marble fireplace. He was all business now. There had been more than enough of this nonsense and he was about to put a stop to it for once and all. He drove straight to the point.

"Why," he demanded in the tone of one who fully expects the correct answer, "is my wife being attacked?"

Jeff shook his head. "I don't know."

Phillips shrugged with impatience. "Come now, let's think this thing out. Obviously the attacker is the person who murdered Austin Marshall. Right?"

"Probably, sir."

"Now, my wife scarcely knew Austin." Jeff sat silent, refusing to enlighten the man concerning his wife's friendship with the victim. "Her only connection with him was through me. Therefore …"

"Therefore," Jeff interrupted, "her only connection with the murder could be through you." Jeff took a step toward him and extended his hand. In it lay the little jeweled elephant. He said, "I think this is yours?"

Phillips picked it up, nodding. "Yes, it's mine. I wear it on my watch chain. I didn't know I had lost it until …"

Jeff said, "You lost it? Then you didn't give it to Mrs. Phillips … weeks ago?"

"No, of course not. Why should she want a thing like this? I was wearing it yesterday. I didn't realize until this morning that I had lost it!" Phillips had dispensed with his calm efficiency now; he was reverting once again to his characteristic air of nervous irritation. "How did you come to have this? What does it all mean, Troy?"

Almost wistfully, Jeff said, "I wish I knew, sir."

"It seems to me, Troy, that for all the snooping and prying you insist upon doing on this case, you know very little!"

"Very little indeed," Jeff said sadly.

"Even that is an overstatement!" Phillips snapped. "I am utterly convinced that you know nothing whatsoever! You have no right to pose as a detective! You are nothing but an impetuous, incompetent young ass!"

Jeff considered that accusation gravely, nodding his head in amiable agreement. "Mr. Phillips," he said eagerly, "I have found out one thing. I do know one thing."

"You flatter yourself, Troy!" Our host was delighted with his own sarcasm. Tasting the words, he repeated them. "You flatter yourself! However, you may proceed."

"Well, this came to me this evening, just before we met your wife in the park. And, strangely enough, it's about you, Mr. Phillips."

"About … about me?"

"Yes. Yesterday, just before Austin Marshall was murdered, you climbed the hill and spoke to him. What did you say to him then? What were you two talking about?"

Phillips' jaw sagged in his surprise at the question. But he quickly recovered and climbed back on the offensive. "What possible difference can that make? Why, we simply chatted, Austin and I. The weather, ship models … I asked Austin if he had decided who was going to represent our club in the International Challenger Trials."

"And had he decided? What did he say?"

"He … come to think of it, I don't remember. I don't believe he told me."

Jeff nodded gravely. "I'm sure he didn't tell you."

William Phillips turned livid; the veins on his forehead and temples stood out in apoplectic ridges.

"Are you," he sputtered, "are you accusing me of ..."

"Yes," Jeff said, "that's right, Mr. Phillips. I'm accusing you of talking to a dead man."

CHAPTER TWELVE

WILLIAM PHILLIPS stood perfectly still, his eyes locked on Jeff, his body painfully rigid. Then he went limp and sank on the edge of his bed. His head wagged foolishly from side to side in unconvincing denial.

"No," he said, "no ..."

"Yes," Jeff said. "When you climbed that hill yesterday to speak to Austin Marshall, you found him dead. You knew immediately that he was dead; you saw that piece of steel sticking out of the back of his neck and you realized that it was murder. Then, instead of raising the alarm, you stood there in front of him, pretending to speak to him, pretending that he was speaking to you. After a minute or two you left him, walked casually down the steps and away from the hill."

"No," Phillips protested weakly. "No, I couldn't have done that, I ..."

"You could do it and you did. But it was too much for you ... that conversation with a corpse. It got you. It made you sick; you collapsed on a bench. Carl Marshall, who was waiting for Penny, saw you and took care of you. He helped you home."

"I ... I asked Carl not to mention that," Phillips mumbled.

"Why shouldn't he?" Jeff asked.

"I told him my wife would worry if she knew I'd been ill. I hoped that would keep him quiet."

"That wasn't smart of you, sir."

"I know, I know," Phillips said dully. "I've done nothing but stupid things since this horrible business began."

"You should have anticipated that Carl's taking you home would be his alibi for the time of the crime. Since everyone, thanks to you, thought Austin had been murdered after you were seen with him, Carl had a perfect alibi. And you could substantiate it for him. Hasn't Hankins been around to ask you to do just that?"

Phillips nodded. "He came to my office this morning. He had accepted Carl's story as an alibi for both of us."

Jeff said, "Didn't he wonder why you needed taking home? Didn't he consider the possibility that the thing which had made you sick was the sight of your friend Austin Marshall with a spike in his neck?"

"No. No, that hadn't occurred to him." Phillips still sat on the edge of his bed, his hand plucking convulsively at the drab quilt. "My plan to switch the time of Austin's murder, however stupid and childish it seems now, might have worked, Mr. Troy. If you hadn't …"

"No," Jeff said. "Hankins would have seen through it sooner or later. I got a break that he didn't. I happened to be at George Mead's yesterday when you refused to offer your perfect alibi. That started me thinking. But Hankins brought your alibi to you straight from Carl. He didn't give you a chance to refuse it, did he?"

"Everything you say is true, everything."

He rose stiffly and walked to a window that was opened only an inch; he closed it. He went to a closet and took down a gray flannel bathrobe. He put it on, huddling himself inside it.

"I've been foolish," he said. "Very foolish."

"What made you do it?" Jeff asked. "Why did you pretend that Marshall was still alive?"

The man was staring unseeingly at a spot on the wall above our heads. He made no move to answer.

Jeff said, "Did you falsify the time of the crime in order to shield someone? The murderer? Mr. Phillips, do you know who killed Austin Marshall?"

The cold eyes left the wall and looked at Jeff. A smile that was more a grimace widened the mouth. "Mr. Troy," he said, "you seem to have reached the extent of your infallibility. No, I do not know who the murderer of Austin Marshall is."

"But you suspect someone?"

"I suspect no one … no certain person."

"But your trick was an obvious effort to confuse the police, to hinder them in solving the case. You don't want this crime to be solved, you don't want the killer to be electrocuted. Why?"

"You're quite wrong. Electrocution is too good for the murderer of Austin."

"All right," Jeff said, "all right. Why did you do what you did?"

"Don't be impatient, Mr. Troy. I am not as young as you … not as quick-witted. Give me a moment, please … just a moment. …"

Phillips had moved to stand in front of one of the bureaus. I could see that the drawer he opened was full of shirts. From its depths he extracted a thin silver flask. He poured from it into its thimble-like cap. I expected him to cough and shudder with distaste when he drank the stuff. He didn't; he relished the drink. He tucked the flask back among the shirts and closed the drawer. He wiped his mouth meticulously with a large white handkerchief, then seated himself in one of the uncomfortable leather chairs.

He cleared his throat and spoke precisely. "When I saw Austin Marshall there on the park bench I knew at once that he was dead … murdered. My first thought, naturally, was of myself. Somehow I had to disconnect myself from this crime, the time and scene of this crime. It was necessary for me to do that because I was not, unfortunately, without a motive to murder Austin Marshall. I might have murdered him because of my wife." Phillips could have been analyzing a stock market trend for all the emotion in his voice; its abstractness was chilling. He went on. "My wife and Austin were not, as I have heretofore intimated to you, mere acquaintances. No, one could hardly have called them mere acquaintances. My wife does not realize that I know that … know that she and my friend Austin were more than acquaintances. …"

I wanted to get out of that room, out of that house. I didn't want to stay and watch the tall gaunt man as he calmly tortured himself. If I could have sympathized with him … but he forbade sympathy; he was enjoying his self-torture.

Jeff stirred uncomfortably on the arm of the chair. "Yes, I see," he said quickly. "You were afraid that the police would find out about Austin and your wife, that they would accept that as your motive for murder. That was why you did it."

"Mr. Troy, do you accept that as a motive for murder?"

"Well, you can't avoid considering it."

"Exactly. You, yourself, prove my fears to be founded. Of course the police would imagine me the killer."

"A suspect," Jeff corrected.

"Very well, a suspect. And even that is ridiculous, really. I was not the least bit concerned over my wife's relationship with Austin. Not in the least."

"You weren't?"

"You find that inhuman of me, Mr. Troy? Let me explain. My wife is of a volatile nature ... over-romantic. This sort of thing has happened before ... once before, and I put a stop to it. Not by murdering the man in question, but by a very simple and civilized device."

"Money," Jeff said.

"Precisely. I made it financially worthwhile for the man to divert his affection from my wife."

"The police, Mr. Phillips, would never believe that you could have bought off Austin Marshall. He didn't need money."

"It would not have been necessary in his case. There is no fear in my mind that my wife would ever have divorced me and gone to Austin. He would not have allowed it. I knew him well; he was not a man to take a woman into his life to the extent of marrying her. He was too self-centered. It would have been a matter of days before Austin would have swept Diane out of his life. So you see, Mr. Troy, it would have all worked out to my satisfaction. Therefore, I had actually no motive for murdering Austin. But I could hardly expect the police to believe that, the police being what they are. And that is why I pretended that Austin was alive when I spoke to him. Now, Mr. Troy, it's very late and I am tired. If you will leave me ..."

It was an effort for him to rise, but he drew himself to his full, awkward height and, bowing stiffly, he dismissed us from the room. As we turned to descend the stairs in the hall, I caught a glimpse of him through the half-open door. He was seated by the dead fireplace, his head bowed on his chest, his hands clutching, as if for support, at the arms of the cold leather chair.

In the foyer the butler popped out of the barrage of mirrors and scurried around us toward the door. Jeff said, "Aw, go to bed, Oswald! I know how to turn a doorknob."

Outside, I said, "Darling, you shouldn't alienate butlers. Some day you might get rich and forget how to open a door."

He grumbled something.

"Jeff, what's wrong with you all of a sudden?"

"I don't want to go up to see Bernard Marshall."

"Do you have to?"

"Yes. Bernard should be able to tell us if his brother was or was not the type to get married."

"Oh," I said, "so you think maybe Phillips was lying."

"Somebody is. Diane says Austin wanted to marry her; Phillips says he didn't."

"Maybe Austin was kidding Diane. You know how some fellows are."

"Well," Jeff said, "I want to find out how Austin was. His little brother should know. I've got to know exactly what Austin's intentions were. If he wasn't going to marry Diane, Phillips doesn't have a motive and there's no need for her to be worried. And if I could eliminate that worry for Diane I'll have earned at least a part of the thousand bucks."

"The thousand bucks," I said. "Don't mention it."

"Haila, I think you're more cut up about that than I am. And I'm the guy who lost it."

There was my chance. My chance to confess to Jeff that I had picked his pocket and put the money where a burglar could find it. I could tell Jeff all, I could be forgiven. Tonight I could sleep instead of twisting and turning till dawn on the sharp, hot tines of my guilty conscience.

"Jeff," I said.

"Yeah?"

"The next time you have that much money," I heard myself saying, "you pin your pocket shut."

"I'll never have that much money again," Jeff said.

In silence we walked to Lexington Avenue and found a taxi.

The rain had tapered to a drizzle, but as we hit the Seventies on Fifth Avenue, it started pouring again. We ducked out of the taxi and up the steps to the front entrance of the Marshall house.

Bernard answered the door himself. His unsurprised and genial greeting eliminated any necessity for an apology over the lateness of our visit or the sodden, mud-splatteredness of our appearance. He smiled and bobbed, he bowed and almost scraped; he seemed to have been wishing for a few people to drop in for a chat.

His manner was gayly charming, but there was something about him that was strange, grotesque. It took me a moment to put my finger on it. The gorgeously quilted maroon dressing gown he wore didn't quite fit the chubby little figure. He looked got-up, masquerade-like. The gown was too long, too wide in the shoulders. When he turned to bow us into the library, I read the answer in the monogram stitched on the breast pocket. Bernard had wasted no time. He was already wearing his dead brother's clothes.

Seating us ceremoniously, he liberally splashed some brandy from an expensive-looking bottle into huge brandy glasses, and passed them around. To Jeff he extended a humidor that would have been desecrated by anything less than a dollar cigar. When Jeff declined, he pressed something extra-special in the way of cigarettes upon us. I didn't get a chance to examine mine until he had lit it for me. Fortunately I hadn't asked him what brand it was. The tiny gold letters engraved on it indicated that it had been made up especially for Austin Marshall. I didn't take another drag of the cigarette; I let it burn itself down between my fingers.

Bernard was now seated in an easy chair, his feet up on a stool. He took a sip of brandy, a long draw on his cigar. His round face glowed, his eyes became mischievous. Bernard was a little boy at home alone; he was doing things he shouldn't do, things he wasn't allowed to do.

"This is nice, isn't it?" he said. "Do you like your brandy?"

"Fine," we said.

"You should like it," Bernard chuckled. "It's the best there is. There's a lot more in the cellar. I'll give you a bottle to take home.

I like liquor, but it doesn't like me."

He giggled.

Jeff said: "Is Carl here?"

"He went to bed long ago. I don't know what's getting into the younger generation. It's just the shank of the evening. Mr. Troy, you're an educated man. What time does the shank start in the evening and what time does it end?"

"It differs," Jeff said. "On the Pacific Coast the shank starts three hours later than here. Mr. Marshall, there are some questions I want to ask you."

"Fire away," Bernard said, "fire away. Mr. Troy, what state has the longest coast line?"

"Florida," Jeff said.

"Your turn, Mrs. Troy!"

"California," I said.

"Michigan!" Bernard chirped triumphantly. "Michigan! Lakes have coasts, not just oceans! Now you ask me one, Mr. Troy!"

"All right," Jeff said. "Was your brother planning to be married?"

"Married? My brother Austin?" Our host's little round eyes popped into big O's. "My brother would never get married, he'd never ..." He stopped speaking. He pulled his feet off the stool and sat on the edge of his chair. Something had happened inside his mind and he was trying to chase the brandy out of it and arrive at some conclusion. We could see him struggling, forcing himself to think. Then he banged his hand down on his knee. He shouted, "Diane Phillips! I thought he was just ... just carrying on with Diane, but no! That's what all that business was about ... he was going to help Diane get a divorce from her husband and he was going to marry her! That's it, that's it! I just realized it now!"

"What made you realize it?" Jeff asked.

"I overheard him talking on the phone to his lawyer. He was talking about divorce ... I know that now. And then Austin was making plans for a trip. He was going to be gone a long time. He was going out west ... to be near Diane, of course, while she was in Reno! Yes, now I can put all those little things that puzzled me together. Austin and Diane!"

"You're positive he was going to marry her?"

"Yes, positive!"

Bernard got up and paced the room; he was excited and, at the same time, pleased. His tipsiness had turned into a new channel; from silliness to a feverish intensity.

"So somebody cracked Austin's shell at last," he crowed. "Austin was always so self-sufficient. He had no time for anyone else's emotions; they bored him."

"What about little Chuckie Clancy?" Jeff asked. "He fussed over Chuckie, he was making him a boat."

"Yes, that's true. He liked children. But, you see, children made no demands on his life, they didn't involve him. And, in a peculiar way, Austin was generous. He overpowered you with his generosity, he never let you forget it. He demanded eternal gratitude from the recipients of his charity." Bernard was turning malicious; he was choosing his words carefully and then spitting them out. "He would have made Diane's life a misery. He would have begrudged her himself, even as little of himself as he would have given her. Diane has been fortunate … very fortunate that Austin was killed before …" He went back to his brandy glass. "I'm … I'm talking too much. We were having such a pleasant time, Mr. Troy, until you brought up the subject of my brother."

"An interesting subject, Mr. Marshall."

"Yes, Austin was interesting." Bernard poured some more brandy. He forced his voice into a festive tone. "Austin was also a good judge of liquor!"

"One more thing!" Jeff said quickly. He was trying to beat the brandy back to Bernard's brain. "Had your brother ever given Tony Gilbert money to produce a play on Broadway?"

Bernard's prolonged chuckle shook his roly-poly little figure. He was delighted that Jeff had asked that question. He seated himself carefully, arranged himself with his glass in one hand, his cigar in the other. He was readying himself to tell a good story. From his attitude it might have been the one about the farmer's daughter.

"Tony Gilbert is the only person I know who ever got the better of my brother. Somehow Tony squeezed fifteen thousand dollars out of him. I suppose he did it with some big talk about how much money a successful play makes. Austin fell for it hook, line and sinker. He handed over the money, just like that!" Bernard's chuckle rose to a new high. "Then Tony never produced the play! I don't think he ever intended to produce it! Austin was furious. He had been made a fool of and he hated it. He's been at Tony about the money ever since. He's threatened him with a lawsuit … but somehow Tony always managed to put him off. It was a treat to listen to Tony. After one of their sessions Austin would be laughing and shaking his hand, almost offering him another loan. Then five minutes after Tony had gone, Austin would be cursing him!"

"Did Tony ever pay any of it back?"

"Not a red cent!"

"Would Austin really have sued him for it?"

"It would have been like him. He hated to be got the better of. When we were boys there was only one thing I could beat my brother at and that was swimming. But I only beat him in a race once. After that I found it was more pleasant to let him win. But here we are again … Austin, Austin, Austin!"

Bernard made a motion at us with the brandy bottle and both Jeff and I said a quick "no." Bernard was wounded; he wanted to have a party, and no one would have a party with him. You could literally watch him slip out from under the influence of his brother and back under the influence of the liquor. He began talking about the season's football. He weighed Yale's chances against Harvard, Harvard's against Princeton, Princeton's against Penn. He went west to the Big Ten. Bernard was a football fan. Each time that we made a move to go he would remember a game that he had seen and that we should know about.

Then a horrible thing happened … Bernard remembered a Dartmouth-Yale game of the early thirties and Jeff became interested. He told Bernard that he had been on the Dartmouth freshman squad that year and that the week before the Yale game they had been running Yale's plays against the Dartmouth Varsity and that on this certain play he was to carry the ball off left tackle. … I put my head on the arm of the chair and closed my eyes as the Varsity coach was telling Jeff that he was sure glad Jeff wasn't playing for Yale against Dartmouth on Saturday. ...

"Haila!" Jeff was shaking me awake.

I sat up and looked around. "Where's Bernard?"

"He passed out all of a sudden. Just as I was telling him why I struck out with the bases full that time in high school. As far as he knows, it was my fault. It wasn't. It was this way. ..."

"How many brandies did you have after I went to sleep?"

"One, Haila. Or two or three."

"What time is it?"

"Two or three."

"Oh, stop saying two or three!"

"All right. See, it was the ninth inning, I was up and the count was two and three on me ... I said two *and* three, Haila. ..."

"Let's go home, Jeff. Please."

"Of course! Nothing's too good for you, Haila."

"Did you put Bernard to bed?"

"Of course. Nothing's too good for Bernard."

"Jeff, I think you're tight!"

"Am I? I was about to ask you if I was."

"And you promised my father you'd never drink!"

"Don't forget that you promised my mother you'd never tell your father if I did. Besides, what do you mean I'm tight? Look!"

I looked, and Jeff was all right. You couldn't tell he'd been drinking. And tomorrow he wouldn't have a hangover. That was the one thing I disliked about my husband. He never had a hangover; I always did.

CHAPTER THIRTEEN

INSOMNIA stalked our bedroom like an irate picket. Jeff tossed and I turned; then I tossed while Jeff turned. That went on and on. The night's last drunk had wended his bleary way down Gay Street; in the milkmen's trucks the empty bottles were beginning to outnumber the full ones; any minute now the worms would start keeping an eye peeled for early birds. And our family's total winks didn't even approach forty, including the nap I had taken at Bernard Marshall's.

In desperation I switched on the light. "Jeff," I said, "this can't go on."

"Oh, I bet it can," he said.

"What's keeping you awake?"

"The clumsy sheep I count keep hurting themselves going over the damn fence. They keep saying 'Ouch' at the top of their lungs."

"Well, lower the fence."

"It isn't mine. Why can't you sleep, Haila?"

"For one thing … Robert Nichols. Who is he? Why did he send us over to Hoboken on a wild goose chase?"

"Yeah, Nichols is doing his bit to keep me awake, too."

"Jeff, were we supposed to still be in Hoboken when that attempt on Diane's life was made tonight? And who fired those shots?"

"Maybe Nichols."

"He didn't look as if he would fire any shots," I said. "He looked like such a nice man."

"Like somebody's father, huh? Little Laura's father, huh? Pardon my hollow laughter."

"You don't really think that he's trying to kill Diane, Jeff?"

"Haila, I'm going to be frank with you. I have no idea who Nichols is, what the hell he is doing, or why. I don't know who's trying to kill Diane or who killed Austin Marshall. I don't know why … well, Haila, I don't know anything. Frankly."

"That isn't quite true, darling."

"I'm warning you! Don't try to cheer me up!"

"No, but you know now that Austin was dead when Phillips talked to him. That was very astute of you, darling, to figure that out."

"Is that what I am … astute? Gee!"

"My, but I'm sleepy!"

"Why don't you take a little nap? Go out in the living room and lie on a loveseat."

"I'm really too sleepy to get out of bed. Good night, Jeff, don't let me sleep more than ten minutes …"

When I awoke a late morning sun was streaming through the venetian blinds, zebra-striping the room. I felt my head for a fevered brow, listened to my breathing for a deathlike rasp and moved my legs to see if they were movable. If after last night's romp in that sopping park, I wasn't an advanced case of double pneumonia, never again would I stand for any unfavorable comparisons of me to the pioneer woman. Me, I thought, I'm rugged, I'm hearty. … I sneezed violently.

What I needed was a cup of something hot. There was nothing wrong with me really, nothing that a cup of coffee wouldn't … The mumble of conversation and the clatter of china sent me flying from my pillow. Uninvited guests were consuming my ration points while I lay abed. I dove into the bathroom, slapped some water in my eyes, cleaned my teeth, skipped massaging my gums, slipped into a housecoat and made for the living room.

The butterfly table had been opened and drawn cozily before the garden windows. My honest-to-goodness Irish linen tablecloth, the one I had been saving for our golden wedding celebration, was spread over it. My precious Limoges that I never washed or dried or even touched for that matter without first praying for Divine Guidance, was set out in full force. And, of course, the only other good things I had, four pieces of Venetian glass, were there. Jeff was entertaining.

Lieutenant Detective Hankins put his coffee cup, not at all gently, on its saucer, and I watched, hypnotized, as it teetered, righted itself, and did not shatter. Assistant Detective Bolling ground out a cigarette on my Venetian glass dessert plate, and I gulped. Jeff shoved back some dishes to make room for the map he was drawing with a fork on my Irish linen tablecloth. By sheer willpower I kept myself from fainting.

I said, "Good morning, fellows."

The fellows stood up and bowed.

"Good morning, Mrs. Troy," Hankins said.

"Good morning, Mrs. Troy," Bolling said. "Won't you sit down and join us in a cup of coffee?"

"Well, now, I might at that, if you insist."

"Would you care for a piece of toast?" Bolling asked. "Troy would be glad to make you some. And maybe a little bacon?"

"You ate all the bacon, Bolling," Jeff said.

"Oh, not all of it!"

"All of it except what I burned," Jeff insisted.

"I'll just have a piece of toast," I said.

"There isn't any more bread," Jeff said. "Bolling ate it all."

"I certainly was hungry, wasn't I?" Bolling observed.

"Well, a cup of coffee will do me," I said.

"There's lots of coffee," Jeff said. He tilted the pot into a cup for me, he tilted and tilted and nothing happened. Finally a tiny trickle of brown stuff covered the bottom of my cup. "That's funny," Jeff said, "I made eight cups. Oh, well, Haila, it would only keep you awake all day."

"I'll make some more," I said.

When I came back from the kitchen, I found the three men immersed in gloomy silence. Jeff's luncheon wasn't going too well. I said conversationally, "How did you all happen to meet up? So early in the morning?"

"Troy was waiting for me at headquarters," Hankins said, "with his story of how Phillips managed to screw us up on the time of the crime."

"Very good work on Troy's part," Bolling said.

"And does it clear up the case?" I asked.

Three faces practically fell into my Limoges.

"Not a bit," Hankins said.

"But it should help, shouldn't it?"

"Yes, Mrs. Troy, it should. Before, when we thought the crime was committed between two-twenty and two-thirty, we had seven witnesses who swore nobody approached Marshall during that time. Now we know that the murder was actually committed between two o'clock, when Marshall climbed the hill, and two-twenty, when Phillips found him dead and pretended he wasn't."

"So now," I said, "you ask your witnesses about *that* time."

"We did," Hankins answered. "We made a grand tour of them this morning."

"But to no avail?"

"No avail at all," Jeff said glumly.

Hankins said, "They've all been concentrating so hard on the time after Phillips talked to Marshall that they can't be sure of anything that happened before then. None of them remembers definitely seeing anyone go up that hill. A couple of them think that maybe some children ran up and down, but that's all."

"Yes," I said, trying to throw my mind back, "there were some children ..." I looked around the table. Six eyes were fastened on my face, full of hopeful pleading. Three heads were inclined toward me, begging me to come through. "I'm sorry," I said, "I can't help either."

"But Haila," Jeff said, "if someone you know now had gone up that hill ... Bernard Marshall or Carl, Penny Mead or her father or Tony Gilbert ... you'd remember that, wouldn't you?"

"Yes, I think so. I'm sure I would."

"I'm sure you would, too. I was sitting there with you and I didn't see anyone go near Austin, damn it."

"It's just like it was," Hankins said. "Nobody saw anybody go near Austin. Anybody except Phillips. Mrs. Troy, you never took your eyes off Phillips while he was up there. Is that right?"

"Yes. If he murdered Austin, he didn't do it on that trip. I would have seen him stab a man in the back of his neck."

"We're right back where we came from," Bolling said. He turned beseechingly to his superior. "There's only one thing left, Hank! Elimination of suspects by means of alibis!"

"Alibis!" Hankins groaned.

"Yes, alibis," Bolling repeated doggedly. "Check and recheck on each suspect. We got to carefully consider ..."

"Listen," Hankins said with infinite patience, "this case isn't going to be solved by alibis or lack of them. All right, all right, I know! The time's different now. The crime was committed between two and two-twenty, not between two-twenty and half-past. It should make a difference ... but it doesn't. Take a look at your suspects. Take Carl Marshall and his uncle Bernard. They were in the park someplace, alone, during the first period ... *and* the second. Take the girl, Penny Mead. She left her father during the first period; she didn't get back until after the second. So both she and her father were alone and unobserved during both periods. Take the actor, Gilbert ..."

"Yeah!" Bolling's eyes glittered. Obviously that was what he had been waiting for. "Yeah, take Gilbert. He says he's got an alibi for the time of the crime. A woman. Even if he won't name her, he's got her up his sleeve and he'll trot her out when he really needs an alibi. Now, look, we get to the woman and ask her exactly what time she met Gilbert. If she says at two o'clock, that eliminates him. But if she says at two-fifteen, it don't eliminate him. And we can trust her because she don't know the real time of the crime. See, if she is lying, she takes care of the time she thinks the crime was committed, between two-twenty and two-thirty. And she would be giving Gilbert an alibi for the wrong time ... Say, is anybody listening to me?"

"I'm not," Hankins said. "No offense, Bolling, it's just a habit of mine."

"But he's got something there," Jeff said. "I was listening to him."

Bolling beamed at him gratefully. "Thanks, Troy. Now, where was I?"

"This woman," Jeff said, "will definitely eliminate Tony or definitely not eliminate him, since we can trust what she says. Because even if she fakes an alibi for him, she'll fake the wrong time."

"Exactly!" Bolling cried. "Because she don't know the right time of Marshall's murder! Nobody does yet except Phillips and us ... and the murderer. And he don't know we know. You understand, Hank?"

"Sure, Bolling, sure. You go right ahead and see this woman. Tell her I sent you."

The assistant detective's chest expansion collapsed. He said morosely, "That's right, we don't know who she is." Then he brightened. "Hank, couldn't we sweat it out of Gilbert?"

"No! Since when can you force someone to give himself an alibi? It's Gilbert's right as a taxpayer to be a murder suspect if he wants to."

"Okay," Bolling said, "I personally will tail Gilbert night and day. Sooner or later he will lead me to the woman. Good-bye, everybody, the next time you see me I will have that woman's name and address, so help me!"

"Wait a minute, Bolling," Jeff laughed. "I'll take care of it for you. I'll see the woman about Tony."

"You know who she is?" Bolling asked.

"You know who she is!" Hankins roared.

"No," Jeff lied quickly. It was a lie, I felt sure, that saved him from being torn asunder. "But I can find out."

"How?"

"Why, I'll ... I'll ask Tony."

Hankins' face turned a mottled red. "Don't you think we asked him?"

"I asked him twice," Bolling said. "It was fruitless."

"He'll tell me," Jeff said. "His mother and my mother belonged to the same high school sorority."

"Troy!" Hankins' fist grazed my Limoges cup as it banged upon the table. "Troy, you're holding out on us! You know who she is right now! I bet you've talked to her already!"

"Sure, he has," Bolling said. "Hank, let's sweat it out of him."

Jeff regarded him with pained disbelief. "Bolling, how could you? I bent over a hot stove for you, I slaved and I ..."

"There's no room for sentiment in the police business," Bolling declared. "Besides, you burned the bacon and the toast was soggy."

"Cut it out!" Hankins bellowed. "Troy, you probably have some damn fool reason for holding out on us, so I'm going to let you get away with it. For a little while."

"As soon as I get the dope on Tony's alibi, I'll let you know."

"All right, Troy, all right. Bolling, are you coming with me or do you want to stay here and help Troy with the dishes?"

"I'll do the dishes," I said quickly. "I like them."

As soon as the two detectives had slammed our front door, Jeff buried his face in the telephone directory and muttered his way through the Davissons, in search of the Walter Davissons on East Sixty-eighth Street. I went into the kitchen and got myself a cup of coffee. I heard Jeff twirl the dial, then wait. He asked to speak with Mrs. Davisson. He listened for a moment. He said a hearty thank you and hung up.

"She's at the broadcasting studio!" he shouted into the kitchen. Then he noticed that I was ten feet away from him at the drop-leaf table, and he lowered his voice. "Her husband's on the air."

"Is it one o'clock already?"

"Quarter after. How long is Davisson's program, Haila?"

"An hour."

"We can catch her then. Want to go with me?"

"I'd love to see the Marriage Doctor in action," I said. "But, Jeff, Marjorie Davisson told us that she was with Tony on Sunday. She's given him an alibi already."

"What time did she say she met him?"

I thought that over. "I guess she didn't, did she?"

"No. I want to know exactly what time they met. To the minute. I owe it to Bolling. Get dressed, Haila."

I was carefully wending my way into my-last-pair-of-nylons when I heard a crash in the kitchen. "Jeff!" I screamed. "Leave the dishes for Mrs. Clancy, don't ..."

"They're all done!" he called.

I met him in the living room. "What did you break? Limoges? Venetian glass? What, which?"

"Huh?"

"I heard you drop something!"

"Oh, yeah, I dropped the dishpan. That isn't Limoges, is it? Put on your shoes. Haila, what's the use of having nice things if you don't use them?"

"Limoges and Venetian glass are practically priceless, darling! That's why I don't use them for everyday ..."

"I meant your shoes. I won't entertain my friends at home any more, Haila. I'll meet them at Nedick's. What station is Davisson's?"

"WQW, the Colonial Broadcasting System, presents the Marriage Doctor daily Monday through Friday at one o'clock. Friends, is your marriage on the brink of disaster? Could you be getting more out of your marriage? Walter Davisson, the noted psychologist ..."

"That's right," Jeff said. "You listen to him, don't you?"

"What do you think makes our marriage run so smoothly?"

"I never look at another woman and Carter's Little Liver Pills. Shall we take the Sixth Avenue Subway?"

The Colonial Broadcasting System had a sixteen story building all its own in the Forties. It was a great slab of smooth gray stone, elegant and imposing. Inside its circular lobby, muraled from the floor to its lighted dome, was a circular desk, covered with oversized morocco-bound, very official looking books. Inside the circle of the desk sat six handsome page boys in maroon and silver uniforms. I went to the nearest one.

"The Marriage Doctor?" I inquired.

He glanced at a clock that was enthroned upon the wall. He consulted one of the books. He said, "Fourteenth floor, Studio B. But the program's on the air, Madam, you're too late to get into the broadcast. There's only eight and a half minutes left. Would you like a ticket for tomorrow's program?"

"We've got to get up there now," I said.

"It's urgent," Jeff said.

"Is it a marital problem?" the youngster asked.

"Oh, yes," Jeff said. "Whenever my wife has guests she locks me in a clothes closet. Then she forgets I'm there and goes away for weekends. What I want to ask the Marriage Doctor is whether there isn't some good substitute for mothballs. The smell of them makes me sick and spoils my weekends. ..."

"You're kidding me," the page said.

"Listen," Jeff said. "Can you get up to Studio B if your marriage is happy? We really want to see the Marriage Doctor's wife."

"Is he married?" the page said incredulously. He turned to one of his colleagues. "Hey, Timmy, did you hear that? The Marriage Doctor has a wife! And I thought he knew all about marriage!"

"That's nothing," Timmy said. "You ever see the You-Too-Can-Be-Beautiful woman? Boy, is she a mess!"

I said, "May we go up and wait for the Davissons?"

"Certainly, Madam. Fourteenth floor, Studio B."

The magnificently attired elevator operator closed the doors, hummed half a bar of a popular song, opened the doors and turned to us.

Jeff said, "We want the fourteenth floor."

"This is it," the operator said.

"Oh," Jeff said. "I thought it was the second."

We stepped out into a tremendous, low-ceilinged lounge. Its floor was completely carpeted in a lush chenille broadloom, its walls upholstered in a soft, gray-tinted linen. Davenports and loveseats and chairs, slipcovered in bright flowered chintzes, formed cozy groups. Low-slung, bleached mahogany tables held crystal ashtrays and the very slickest of magazines. The whole room was lighted softly by a marvel of indirection.

A bespectacled young man with a loaded briefcase on his lap and the defiant look of the unarrived genius on his face sat on the edge of a chair, probably waiting for some program director to tell him that his scripts were not commercial. Two girls fidgeted nervously on a davenport, probably awaiting an audition. Another girl, bored and sophisticated, sat calmly smoking a cigarette. She was undoubtedly the actress who played the title role in *Elvira of Welcome Valley*. In the far corner, a page boy worked behind a desk.

None of them was listening to the WQW program that was being piped into the lounge for their edification and amusement. The overripe voice of an announcer was saying, "And now we have the case of Mrs. L.G. Mrs. L.G., may I present Mr. Davisson, the Marriage Doctor."

At the other end of the room two neon signs informed us that Studio A was to the right, Studio B to the left. A, the bright letters went on to say, was in rehearsal; B was on the air. We walked through the lounge toward the signs.

"Mr. Davisson," a tremulous, high-pitched voice was telling the world, "my husband and I have been married now for eighteen years. In those eighteen years there has never been a cross word or an inharmonious thought between us. That is, until last week. Last week, Mr. Davisson, my husband …"

I peeked to the right to see what was rehearsing in Studio A. Through a large rectangular window I saw the pantomime of a silent orchestra playing its head off. Jeff and I stopped to watch. It was an eerie feeling standing there, watching an orchestra play music that you couldn't hear while you listened to a voice whose owner you couldn't see.

"And so, Mrs. L.G.," the Marriage Doctor's soft, confidence-inspiring voice was saying, "this is my advice to you. Both you and your husband have too many things in common, too great a bond of understanding between you, too many joys and heart-aches to let a thing like this ..."

We turned and approached the window of Studio B. The room behind it was semicircular in shape with about ten rows of seats rising slightly from the small stage at the far end. It was a packed house, its audience all women except for one unfortunate who twiddled his thumbs and stared at the floor. A few rows in front of him sat Marjorie Davisson. She was leaning back in her chair, completely at ease, a tiny satisfied smile curving her unpainted lips. Her bright head nodded in pleased agreement with her husband's counsel.

"... so don't let any quarrel, important as it may seem now, ruin these many wonderful years that you have already had and the many more that can be ahead of you. Go to your husband, is my advice, talk to him as you have to me, tell him ..."

Jeff and I edged closer, to a spot where we could command a clear view of the stage. On a row of straight-backed chairs sat the women whose marital problems were being aired and solved by Walter Davisson. There were two desks, each equipped with a microphone. At one sat the announcer, a sheaf of papers in his hand. At the other, speaking to a buxom, sad-eyed woman, sat a little man with pale blue eyes and a fringe of sandy hair. On the corner of his desk was a hat, a gray hat, so new that it made his clothes seem old.

I grasped Jeff's arm and squeezed it.

Walter Davisson, the Marriage Doctor, was Robert Nichols.

CHAPTER FOURTEEN

WE STOOD back from the doorway while the mob of chattering women surged out of Studio B. Somehow, even in a crowd Marjorie Davisson managed to give the impression that she was walking with her long, swinging tread. She wore a deep yellow linen suit and her soft bright hair curled up over a tiny yellow beanie. The faint smile still played about her lips; she was oblivious of the excited wives who were milling around her.

Jeff moved toward her and touched her on the arm. The smile disappeared, but only for a moment. Then it was back again in its full, friendly radiance. She thrust out her hand and took Jeff's. She extended the other to me.

"How nice!" she said. "The Troys! I didn't see you in the audience or I would have sat with you."

"We got here too late to get in," Jeff said.

"Oh, I'm sorry. Walter was especially good today. It's really miraculous how he handles those hysterical women."

"I'd like to meet your husband, Mrs. Davisson."

"I don't know …" She looked back toward the stage; by now the crowd had thinned enough for us to see it. It was empty. "I'm afraid Walter's gone. He sneaks away the minute the program's over. He has to, you know. Otherwise, he'd be deluged with questions. And he doesn't know I'm here today, so he's probably …"

She stopped speaking to us because she realized we had stopped listening to her. She turned to see why. Out of a door, upholstered to match the lounge walls and invisible when closed, stepped Walter Davisson … better known to us as Robert Nichols, father

134

to a phantom girl in phantom trouble. His smiling, pale blue eyes searched the crowd, found his wife and grew more smiling, lit on us and blinked. Three papers fluttered from his hand, suddenly gone limp. He licked his lips in the same worried manner that Robert Nichols had moistened his the day before. And then he took a deep breath and held it as he stood waiting for us to approach him.

Marjorie was concerned. "Walter," she said, "what's wrong? Are you ill? You've been overworking. ..."

"Hello, Mr. Nichols," Jeff said.

The man tried to smile and missed. His wife looked at Jeff, wide-eyed. "Mr. Nichols?" she said. "You don't understand, Mr. Troy ... this is my husband."

"That," said Jeff, "is what he tells you. He's got a wife in Texas. And a grown daughter here in New York. We found your daughter, Mr. Nichols. She's waiting for you down at our apartment."

"Please, Mr. Troy, please!" Davisson looked about him anxiously. "I owe you an explanation, I realize that. I ... come with me, I'll ..."

He darted down the length of the lounge, keeping far enough ahead of us to make conversation impossible. He almost broke into a run when a woman, waiting before an elevator, made a move toward him. Marjorie, Jeff and I followed in single file. Davisson opened a door, held it while we passed him and entered a small library. He closed the door quietly and stood with his back against it.

"This is all right," he said. "We will be able to talk here." His voice was strangely alien to the one that came over the air. For one thing, it was his diction. The studied, almost British speech he used in broadcasting he dropped in private conversation. Now he slurred his words, looping them together in running sentences. Then, too, the microphone affected the quality of his voice, deepened its tone, strengthened its timbre, making it sound profound. Walter Davisson, unaided by a mike, would have no more power over an audience than yesterday's Robert Nichols would have had. "I hope you'll be patient with me, Mr. Troy," he went on, "for I have an explanation that I'm sure will ... will justify my strange behavior."

"Walter!" Marjorie said, her hands fluttering in midair. "What's happened? I don't understand!"

"Please, Marjorie, this is difficult enough for me." Davisson faced Jeff again. "Mr. Troy, I ... I'm glad to know that you have a sense of humor ..."

"Yeah," Jeff said. "You should have seen me last night in Hoboken, soaked to the skin and doubled up with laughter."

"Ah, but saying you had found my daughter!" Mr. Davisson worked his way through an anemic chuckle. "That shows you do have a sense of humor."

"Make me laugh some more. Tell us all about it. Why did you do what you did? Besides wanting to see if I had a sense of humor?"

Davisson wiped his face with his handkerchief, thoroughly, meticulously. He refolded it, replaced it in his breast pocket. "Mr. Troy," he said, "my action yesterday was to be the beginning of a long campaign. I would have made contact with you today, tomorrow and the next day. Unfortunately, you came here and now it's finished. My reason for this campaign is as simple as it is important ... important to me. I hoped, and I succeeded to a point, to interest you in the case of a girl in danger. I hoped that you would work on it so much that you would find no time for anything else. The anything else being, specifically, the Austin Marshall murder. I wanted you to stop investigating that case."

"You went to a lot of trouble," Jeff said.

"It was worth it. It would have been worth much more to me. It is of the most extreme importance to me that a certain fact ... a fact which you were already heading toward ... never be made public. Please do not ask me what that fact is."

"I won't," Jeff said. "I'm barely on speaking terms with you, brother."

"You may discover this fact sooner or later; I shan't be able to prevent that now. In your investigation of the Marshall case you may uncover what I would do anything to keep hidden."

Marjorie Davisson stamped her foot in physical impatience. "I can't stand this any longer!" she cried. "Walter, what in God's name did you do?"

He regarded his wife with a mixture of reproof and pain. He seemed about to be severe with her. Instead, he sighed, dismissed his disapproval and said matter-of-factly: "Yesterday, Marjorie, I took matters into my own hands. When you told me that Mr. and Mrs. Troy had been to see you about the murder, I wanted to call on them. You said I couldn't, that they wouldn't be at home. They had told you where they were going, however. They had to be at Beekman Place, they said, at five o'clock."

"Yes. Yes, but, Walter, you didn't ..."

"I did. I went to Beekman Place. I saw Mr. and Mrs. Troy go into a house there and immediately come out again. I watched them walk away, I ... I followed them. I didn't speak then because I hadn't yet planned any course of action. I didn't know how to approach them. They went into a bar on Third Avenue and there I overheard them talking to a woman. I gathered that it was she who had hired Mr. Troy to work on the Marshall case. That gave me my idea. I would hire Mr. Troy myself ... to work on another case. And I would make my case so desperate and so urgent that he would be unable to resist it."

"You were irresistible, all right." Jeff had tired of being irate; a grin cracked his face. "Haila and I rushed over to Hoboken. You had me feeling like Dick Tracy."

Davisson leaped with a great relief at the change in Jeff's attitude. The worry dropped from him; a pleasure at his own cleverness took its place. He began to enjoy himself, like a boy boasting of a successful Halloween prank.

"Yes," he smiled, "I did rather a good job of acting, didn't I? But how did you discover, Mr. Troy, that I was hoaxing you?"

"You talked about being on the second floor at 479 Pine Street. That house is a one-story job."

"Is it, really?" Davisson chuckled. "I knew there was a Pine Street in Hoboken, but I selected a number at random. I hoped there would be a house there. So there was one, was there? And what did the people there make of your quest for Laura?"

"The people there," Jeff said, "almost made the trip worthwhile. A wonderful couple who will never bother you with any marital problems, Doctor. They're not married. They had a fine time taking us for a ride about Laura. Mr. Davisson, if we had come back from Hoboken still believing you, what …"

"Ah, yes! I had my next move planned. I was going to tell you that I had had further communication from my daughter. That she had been taken from Hoboken to a downtown hotel. Your search of the downtown hotels, I hoped, would keep you too busy to work on the Marshall case for quite some time."

"Walter, no! No, no, no!" Marjorie Davisson was gasping for breath. Then she stopped struggling and a burst of uncontrolled laughter poured out of her. "Oh, dear," she finally managed to say, "I can't stand it! Walter, you did all that … you went through that wild, fantastic business all for nothing!"

"As it turned out, yes. But I didn't expect Mr. Troy to appear at the studio here this afternoon. And I didn't expect the house in Hoboken to be a one-story building. I thought the people there would merely disclaim any knowledge of Laura and that Mr. Troy would think they were lying and …"

"I don't mean that!" She was sponging her eyes with a square of yellow linen. "I don't mean that at all. Mr. and Mrs. Troy know, Walter. They've known all along the thing that you've taken such fabulous pains to hide."

The Marriage Doctor gaped incredulously at his wife; she had done something beyond his wildest imagining. He could hardly voice his feeling. "But, Marjorie, you told me … you swore to me that Mr. Troy … that nobody knew about you and Gilbert …"

"You frightened me into lying to you. I was afraid if you found out that the Troys knew, you'd do something absurd." Mrs. Davisson smiled wryly. "It worked the other way, didn't it? You didn't know that they knew and you did something absurd to keep them from finding out."

"You two," Jeff said, "ought to get together."

"It's all my fault," Marjorie said.

"It is indeed!" her husband said angrily.

"Perhaps not!" Marjorie flared. "If you hadn't so suspiciously third-degreed that eavesdropping maid of ours and discovered that I had been called upon by a detective, everything would be all right now! If you hadn't been so furious with me I wouldn't have been afraid to tell you the truth … I would have told you that I had explained my connection with Tony to the Troys!"

"There is no excuse for lying …"

"Oh, don't be sanctimonious, Walter! It was such a tiny lie!" She turned to Jeff. "I told Walter that you had called on me simply because you knew I sailed my boats in the park every day and that I had been there around the time of the murder. I just skipped telling him that you had seen me take a note from Tony's boat and wanted to know all about me and Tony. It was simply a little sin of omission to keep peace in our family …"

Davisson stopped her with a look. His meek round face burned with outrage. His speech became the weighted tones he used before a microphone.

"Marjorie," he said, "this stupid, ridiculous, juvenile business between you and Gilbert must end! However innocent it actually is does not matter; it is beside the point. Your surreptitious meetings and your sly exchange of notes would seem nothing but clandestine and scandalous to anyone who does not know you as I do!"

"Darling," Marjorie faltered, "you're absolutely right …"

Walter Davisson thundered on. "If this asinine story came to light at any time, it would be bad enough! But in connection with a murder … it would be a front page scandal! You know what that would do to me, Marjorie! I would be laughed off the air! This business of mine may seem trivial to you, but I've spent nearly a lifetime …"

"I know, Walter, I know! And I'm sorry. But Mr. Troy has promised he won't tell anyone about Tony and me."

Davisson looked at Jeff, looked hopefully, searching for some evidence that he was a man of his word. Jeff did his best.

"I don't see any reason," he said staunchly, "why anyone should know about this, Mr. Davisson."

"But the police, what about them?"

"I'll handle that for you. In fact, that's why I'm here now. Tony has told the police that he was with a woman at the time of the crime, but he gallantly refuses to give the name of the woman. I'll check Tony's alibi with Mrs. Davisson and tell the police about it without mentioning her name."

"You see, Marjorie," Davisson groaned, "this is all so shoddy, so … I don't like it. Mr. Troy, I owe you a great deal. If there were only some way I could repay you."

"Just don't arrange any more trips for Haila and me," Jeff said. "Mrs. Davisson, on Sunday afternoon you met Tony, downtown, you said."

She nodded. "Yes. In front of his theater. We wandered around for a few minutes. We had a drink at Longchamps together."

"And you met him about half-past two?"

"Oh, no. Much earlier. We had planned to meet at two sharp, but he was a few minutes late. It was close to five after two when he arrived."

"How long were you together?"

"Not more than fifteen minutes. Tony had to make up for his performance. I left him at about twenty after …" Her face went blank before it flooded with alarm. "That … that *is* an alibi for him, isn't it? Oh, I know that Mr. Marshall was killed between two-twenty and half-past, but Tony could never have got all the way back to Central Park in time to … he couldn't have!"

"It doesn't matter whether he could have or not," Jeff said. "We know now that Austin Marshall was dead by two-twenty."

"But I thought …"

"So did we. We were wrong."

"Well then, since Tony was with me until two-twenty …"

"Yes," Jeff said. "You're an alibi for him."

"See, Walter!" she cried. "Some good has come out of my friendship with Tony!"

"Hmm," Davisson grunted.

"But if it weren't for me, Tony would be …"

"Yes, Marjorie, yes, I know, I know! So the two of you had a drink together at Longchamps! Such a rash thing to do! What if you had been seen by some gossip columnist? Tony is an actor, you are the wife of a man fairly prominent in radio. Both of you are of some news value to columnists. Marjorie, you must never see Gilbert again. Never."

"Never, dear," Marjorie said meekly. "Never again."

"I mean it this time!"

"And so do I! I do, truly!" She turned quickly to us. "I can't thank you enough for everything …"

"Oh, no, you don't!" Jeff shook a finger at her. "Your husband wants to give you a good scolding and we're not going to let you hide behind us. Come on, Haila. Mr. Davisson, before you beat your wife make sure these walls are soundproof. Unless you want to audition for a sponsor."

We got into an elevator, fell to the lobby floor and walked toward the Fifth Avenue entrance. Jeff was smiling happily. I didn't blame him. We had had a pretty good hour. One: cleared up the mystery of the lost Laura and the noxious Nichols. Two: eliminated Tony, thereby changing Bolling's theory to fact. All in all, not a bad hour. Except, of course, that there still remained the little matters of who murdered Austin Marshall and who tried to murder Diane Phillips.

"Jeff," I said, "let's phone Diane. Just to see if she's up and about."

"We'll call her from my studio. I want to go up there and tell the boss I still work for him. …"

Jeff darted away from me and around a corner into the landing and taking-off area of the local elevators. When I caught up to him, he was talking to Tony Gilbert. The actor, dressed as if he were going to lecture a woman's club, was shaking his head in protest.

"No, Jeff," he said, "I didn't see you. Haila, your husband thinks I was trying to avoid you two. Tell him how I feel about you, Haila. I'd walk a mile of tightrope to see you … even with this big lug around your neck."

"Tony," Jeff said, "you might as well go home."

"Why?"

"Marjorie Davisson won't be meeting you. Mr. Davisson has put his foot down. No more Tony for Marjorie. We just heard the ultimatum upstairs."

"Is Marjorie up there?"

"Cut it out, Tony."

"No, really! I'm here to audition for a soap opera … Happiness Highway or Life Need Not Be So Sordid, something like that. Did you say a foot was put down? Davisson's foot?"

"He put it right down on your neck." Jeff told him about Marjorie's promise never to see him again. Tony was not saddened in the least by the news. In fact, he was delighted. I could see him accept the challenge of Davisson's dictum. Jeff saw it, too, and laughed. "What will you do now, Tony? Buy yourself a rope ladder?"

"It's an interesting problem, isn't it? It'll take a little thought. Excuse me while I go someplace to think."

"Wait, Tony," Jeff said. "Austin Marshall was a hard, hard man, wasn't he?"

"I don't get you."

"A man who hated to be owed money. Especially if he thought his money had been squandered. But you don't get me."

"Oh, that!" Tony snapped his fingers.

Jeff snapped his, too. "Fifteen thousand bucks. You can get change for it in any cigar store. Marshall told you to forget it, huh? He'd write it off his income tax."

"Who's been talking to you about that?"

"Someone sent me a note about it … in a boat."

Tony laughed. "I'm glad you brought that up. Didn't Marjorie give me an alibi?"

"A fine one," Jeff admitted.

"Well, then, why are you trying to line up a motive for me?"

"I don't know why I do things. I'm not mental, I'm emotional. A fortune teller told me once never to use my mind."

"Look, Jeff, I wouldn't kill a man for fifteen thousand dollars … that I'd already spent. That isn't good economics."

"But if Marshall was getting tough about it? I gather you practically swindled him."

"I did? Listen, Marshall hardly ever bothered to ask me about that money. When he did, it was like a guy saying when are you going to pay me back that two bucks you owe me? That's all fifteen thousand meant to him."

"Pin money."

"Sure, Jeff." Tony laughed some more. "Pin money, and he got stuck with it. But he didn't care. Want me to cross my heart? No,

I can't, can I? Marjorie Davisson has my heart. I think I had better leave you two. I want to jot down all these things I'm saying, they're rich! I ought to write for radio and I think I will. So long."

Tony ducked into an elevator and the doors closed between us. We walked to another elevator, in the Graylock Building a dozen blocks away, and rode up to Jeff's presumable place of business. We didn't get as far as the boss. The boss' secretary stopped us with a message for Jeff. A Mr. Bernard Marshall had telephoned; he wanted to see Mr. Troy at his earliest convenience.

Our Fifth Avenue bus, one of those ancient ones which deserved by now to be turned out to pasture, groaned and jerked its way up through the Fifties and Sixties and on into the smoother-going Seventies. The park, appearing very chipper after its drenching of the night before, was dutifully playing host to the preschool-aged kiddies. On the knoll across the lake three tots were sitting on Austin Marshall's bench while a white-clad nurse read to them.

"It's a shame," Jeff said, "about Tony. He can't have any more fun sending notes to Marjorie. He'll have to sail empty ships."

"Mr. Davisson is an old meanie to discontinue such a romantic postal system. Darling, your love letters to me weren't delivered so romantically, but they didn't sound like travelogues. Yours was a passionate pen."

"A passionate Corona Standard portable."

"It's just too bad about Tony and Marjorie. I suppose their date for Thursday night is off now, too. I wonder where Tony Quixote would have walked his lady love on Thursday. Maybe they would have strolled hand-in-hand through the needle trade district, down to the financial section and then … Hey, we get off here!"

The Marshall house looked as monstrously gloomy bathed in bright sunshine as it did in the dark of night. Its heavy gables and foreboding shutters seemed to be giving the sun the cold shoulder, daring it to shine through a window. The wizened old-lady servant answered our ring, but before any words could be exchanged, Bernard Marshall trundled into the hall.

"Mr. Troy," he said, "I'm glad you got my message." His face shone with beads of sweat. "I had to talk to you at once."

"You seem worried, Mr. Marshall," Jeff said.

"Yes, I am. Something terrible ... something I never thought possible ... I wish I didn't have to tell you."

"But you do have to?"

"Oh, yes, I can't do otherwise. I would get into trouble ... I mean, it's against the law and then, of course, Austin was my brother. You see," he sighed, "I know who ... who killed him."

"Oh," Jeff said.

CHAPTER FIFTEEN

Austin Marshall's brother stood before us, his baby-plump hands fanned out as he tapped the finger tips against each other in a nervously uncertain gesture. He started to speak again and changed his mind. He fidgeted for a moment longer. Then, with a painful shrug of resignation, he turned away from us.

"If you'll come with me, please," he said.

We followed the stubby figure as it waddled through the dark cavernous hallway. Great cold statues and dim brown-black portraits formed a gauntlet for their small owner and seemed to dwarf him even more with their ponderous dignity. Thick dreary carpets swallowed the sound of our footsteps.

At the end of the hall Bernard threw open the door to the hobby room that had been Austin's pride and joy, and then stepped back to let us enter. One step inside the room we stopped short. It was not empty. Against the workbench in the corner leaned Diane Phillips. There was only one word to describe the Diane who stood before us. It was frightened.

Beneath the drawn pallor of her skin the black, high-necked dress she wore lost its expensive chicness. It had a shroud-like look about it. There were purple hollows under Diane's eyes and the wide, gay mouth that she had painted on with scarlet rouge looked grotesquely artificial.

She tried to smile a greeting at us. She said, "Bernard, you've told them ..."

"No," he said. "I … I thought it better if …" He turned to us and waved his hand in the direction of some chairs. His relief at the necessity for this one small gesture was obvious. If social amenities would postpone the crisis that seemed to be approaching only for a moment, then Bernard Marshall was all for social amenities.

I sat down, but Jeff didn't. He stood leaning against the wall just inside the door, his eyes fastened on Diane Phillips.

She said, "I … I asked Bernard to call you. It's because of me that he did. I have something to tell you that …" She stopped, swallowing painfully. Her hands tightened as they clung to the edge of the workbench. In a hard, dry voice, she said, "Bernard. Bernard, please."

He fumbled for a moment. Then, when he finally began, he spoke rapidly, racing through words to get them said and done. "Diane has come to me with a … an amazing story. You know the facts … how someone attacked her in her house, how someone shot at her in Central Park. The feeling she has had of being watched and followed … you know all that. She has told me, too, why she hired you to work on this case. She was afraid that suspicion for my brother's murder would fall unjustly on her husband. Therefore I felt that you should know at once … to help us, to advise us …" Bernard took a deep breath, dragging it in. "Diane is now convinced," he blurted, "that her husband is the murderer. That he killed Austin."

With a hand that trembled the little man wiped his forehead. He was panting as if he had just finished a mile run. He sank down into a chair and peered from Jeff to Diane.

Jeff hadn't moved. He was looking hard at the woman. "Then you think," he said at last, "that it is your husband who is trying to murder you?"

Her answer was so soft that I could hardly hear it. "What … what else am I to think? If William murdered Austin, then …"

There was absolute quiet in the room. It lasted for one minute, two, three … it lasted until I could almost feel Austin Marshall's presence among us there. I could see his tall, thick figure before the shelves of books on model yachting and model railroads and cryptography. I could see his dark head bent over his stamps and his coins, see him at his workbench building a ship for his small friend, Chuckie Clancy. Bernard Marshall seemed to feel it, too. He stirred uneasily and glanced about him with the look of a trespasser.

It was Jeff who finally broke the pounding silence. He said to Diane, "Why are you so sure of your husband's guilt now? What proved it to you so suddenly?"

She flung out her arms with a desperate helplessness. "You know what proved it to me. The same thing that must have proved it to you. I didn't fool you last night, I didn't convince you. You knew that I was lying to shield William. I didn't drop the gold elephant there. William was wearing it on Sunday when Austin was killed. I saw it on his watch chain when he left to go to the park. I saw that it was gone when he came home. Austin must have clutched at it and torn it off his watch chain. It … it must have fallen from Austin's hand when he … when he died. You figured that out, didn't you? You must have known that!"

"Then you lied to me last night? You did find the elephant near the park bench just before we came?"

"Yes, Jeff."

He looked at her and shook his head. "No, Diane."

Her eyes, suddenly panic-stricken, flew to his face. "Yes … yes, I tell you …"

Jeff was still shaking his head. "No, Diane. On a dark, rainy night you didn't find a thing that the police missed in broad daylight. You didn't discover a clue in a few moments in a spot that the police had combed for hours. But you hoped that I'd think you'd found it there. You wanted me to think that you were lying last night, that you were shielding your husband. You knew that that would make him look much guiltier than anything else you could do."

She was crouched against the workbench now, her fist beating savagely against its top. "No … no! Why should I do a dreadful thing, a horrible thing like that!" The denial was spit out. "Why should I!"

"I'll tell you why," Jeff said. "Maybe, to put it mildly, because you dislike your husband. You want to see him convicted of this crime. That's why you paid me to investigate this case and then deliberately threw evidence at me that would damn him. That phony attack on you in your house … no one could possibly have attacked you but William. The confession you made of your relationship with Austin … which gave William a motive for murder. The business last night … having someone phone you at our house, knowing that I would follow you and find you with William's charm in your hand. And all the time you played the loving, frightened wife, terrified that your husband would be found guilty of a crime you were trying your damnedest to pin on him. You hired me as a medium between you and the police because you were afraid to pull your act on them. It was less dangerous with me; I'm not the law."

Bernard Marshall struggled to his feet, his pink face flooded with a fiery red. "This … a mistake," he said, gasping. "This … it's incredible!"

"Incredible," Jeff said, "but true. It is true, Diane, isn't it?"

She looked at him bitterly and switched her gaze to Bernard. It was his face that broke her. He was still mumbling protestations, still whispering a feeble defense of Diane. But the words were incongruous with his feelings that were written so clearly in his eyes. There was a certain knowledge of the truth there, there was bewilderment at Diane's deceit and disgust at her tactics.

She had caught the full impact of his verdict in a brief flash. Slowly, in a monotone, she said, "Yes. All right. I did everything you say. I've lied and cheated and connived with all that was in me to prove him guilty. I'd give my life to have it that way." The deadly, controlled voice broke and rose in a harsh hysteria. "But he killed him, William killed him! He did it because I loved Austin, because he didn't want me to go to him! He'd do anything to keep me chained to him. Once before there was someone. It was Tony Gilbert. I wanted to leave William then, and he stopped me. He bought Tony off, bought him off with money! But he couldn't have bought Austin! There was no way for him this time but murder. And he murdered Austin!"

Bernard moved toward her and reached out his hand to touch

her arm beseechingly. "Diane," he pleaded, "Diane, try to control yourself. This ... this doesn't help."

She shrugged him off viciously, her eyes on Jeff. "I never loved William, you know. I knew that I didn't almost as soon as I married him. It was a horrible mistake ... we both knew it. But he wouldn't admit it, he wouldn't let me go. He knows how I loathe him, that doesn't matter to him. Nothing matters except that he keep me chained to his side all the rest of my life. And now ... now he's even murdered to keep me there."

Jeff shook his head. "You haven't proved that your husband is the murderer, Diane. Everything against him has been manufactured by you. There isn't anything ..."

She interrupted him fiercely. "But those shots last night! You were there, you know! Oh, I did all the rest, I've admitted to it all. But not that! I didn't fake those shots, I swear I didn't! How could I have done that!"

"You couldn't have," Jeff confessed.

"It was William who shot at me, who tried to kill me! Can't you see that? He killed Austin and now he will murder me. He'll murder me because I know he's guilty, because I know ..."

She buried her face in her hands and sank into a chair. Dry, strangled sobs shook her body. Bernard started toward her again and stopped. Then he turned and moved on tiptoe toward the door, beckoning for us to follow.

In the hall outside he said, "I'll take care of her, Mr. Troy. It's better, I think, if you go." He opened the door for us.

Jeff slid his hand to the knob and closed it again. He said, "Wait a minute. There's something I want you to tell me first. It's about Austin. Did he wear glasses only for reading?"

The round fat face showed no surprise at Jeff's question. He had only half-listened to it. His eyes were fighting the dimness of the hall, straining toward the door we had just come through. We could still hear the helpless sobbing behind it.

"Yes," he said vaguely, "yes, only for reading. No other time."

"You're certain of that?" Jeff prodded.

"Of course." A note of impatience crept into the vacant voice. "Austin was very vain about that." Once again he moved to open the door, and once again Jeff stopped him.

He said, "There's something else, Mr. Marshall. When your brother's body was examined, was any reading material found on it? You know … letters … a pocket edition … notes of any sort?"

"No, nothing at all." A flicker of interest showed in Bernard's face. "Why do you ask this?"

"It may help," Jeff told him. "Thank you."

On our way home, Jeff said only five words. I couldn't figure out any whys or wherefores for them, and he uttered them with a positiveness that made my bafflement complete.

"Diane," he said, "is in no danger."

When we reached number thirty-nine Gay Street, Mrs. Clancy's daily bulletin was in Jeff's typewriter.

"Mr. Troy," the message read, "Mr. Wm Phillips wants you to meet him at four at Austin Marshall park bench. He said you would know. He said you should come alone."

Jeff read it and stuffed the paper in his pocket without comment. For the next half hour, still without comment, he prowled around the house in the throes of thought. Troy in the throes of thought was a terrifying sight. He would halt abruptly in midstep and stand frozen, staring right through me or anything else that happened to be in his line of vision. Then a satisfied smirk would turn his mouth up at the corners, or a silent and horrible curse would turn it down. His pacing would continue then, getting faster and faster as his excitement grew. He had added a pack of half-smoked cigarettes to our already overflowing ashtrays. Now he was lighting matches, reaching into his pocket for a cigarette that wasn't there, forgetting to blow out the match until it burned him.

I was close to the screaming point when he snatched up his hat and headed for the door. The hour for his meeting at the Austin Marshall park bench had arrived. I dragged him to a stop just before he slammed out.

"Jeff," I said, "I'm not going to sit down here all alone. I'll go up and call on Penny Mead. You come there when you've finished with Phillips."

He nodded.

"Jeff," I said, "are you hearing me?"

He nodded again.

"Be careful crossing streets, darling, in your condition. Get a policeman to help you across."

He looked at me and laughed. He had been able to figure out something about Austin Marshall's murder. He kissed me, but perfunctorily. He had not been able to figure out everything about it.

From the front window I watched him as he swung out of sight around Gay Street's elbow. Then I changed my clothes, my makeup and my hairdo, and started for Penny Mead's.

The subway train was approaching my stop at Fifth Avenue and Fifty-third Street. I was caught in a little jam at the door when I saw the man's wallet. His face was buried in a folded newspaper, his coat was hanging open. I was standing close enough to him to be able to see the wallet clearly. I had picked my own husband's pocket with success; this would be a cinch. I could jostle against him accidentally, push the paper in his face, pick the wallet out of his pocket. I could charmingly beg his pardon, smile at him winningly, and walk away with his money. There might be a lot of money in that wallet; there might be as much as a thousand dollars. ...

Horrified by my thoughts, I wrenched my gaze away from the man. Had my one excursion into crime been my undoing? Had it been habit-forming? Had I turned already into an inveterate pickpocket? I was shaking like a leaf. From now on would temptation such as this be more than I could stand. ...

Before I realized what I was doing, I had raised my hands to the man's coat. I quickly buttoned it. He dropped his paper and stared at me in amazement.

"Pardon me," I gasped, "but you ... you'll catch cold!"

The subway doors were opening. I fled.

The butterflies in my stomach didn't stop fluttering until I saw the benign, comforting face of the Mead butler. He bowed me in and took my coat. "Is Miss Mead in?" I asked.

From the next room an unmistakable voice bellowed at me. "Haila Troy, come in here, girl! Come in here this minute!"

I found George Mead sitting rigidly in his wheelchair, pounding the arms of it with clenched fists. His face was a thunder-cloud.

"They've done it!" he shouted. "The base ingrates have done it! They ... they ..." He sputtered himself into speechlessness.

"Who, Mr. Mead, has done what?"

He tried to roar the answer at me and went immediately into a paroxysm of coughing. While he straightened himself out with a glass of water from the chromium bottle at his side, I tried to ease his embarrassment by looking out a window. It faced the Avenue, the height of the building cutting the street from view, and Central Park stretched itself out like a green map beneath me. There was the lake, looking like a small blue lozenge from my altitude. There was the rocky pinnacle beside it. And there was a solitary and familiar figure sitting on its top. William Phillips had not yet arrived; Jeff waited alone at the scene of the crime.

Behind me George Mead was shouting again. "By Jupiter, I nearly died just now! That's what they've done to me ... killed me! Girl, Penny and Carl Marshall have eloped! They're married!"

"That's fine, Mr. Mead! Congratulations!"

"Penny's gone! Forever!"

"Forever?"

"Yes! She won't be back until Saturday!"

I started to laugh. George Mead glared at me furiously; then he was chuckling and slapping his thigh. "Girl, that Penny of mine is a chip off the old block! Just like me! Makes up her mind to do a thing and hell can't stop her! Defied me, by God! Give me a cigarette, girl, I'm fresh out!"

I opened my purse, handed him a cigarette and lit it for him. Then I moved to drop the burnt match in an ashtray. And I stood, the match still in my hand, looking at the tray, fascinated by it, not knowing why.

There was nothing unusual about it. A big crystal bowl filled to the brim with ashes and stubs and burnt matches. It was very like one of ours ... the one in which Jeff had snuffed out his innumerable cigarettes while he ran his mental marathon this afternoon. That was it. It wasn't George Mead's ashtray that had given me the feeling that something was indefinably and terribly wrong. There was nothing strange about this tray that I stood looking at now; there had been something wrong with ours.

I closed my eyes in a frantic effort to reconstruct our living room as Jeff and I had walked into it. There had been a newspaper on the floor; I had picked it up. A magazine bookmarked with the arm of a chair. Two dirty glasses on the coffee table. Ashtrays filled with the crushed butts of cigarettes. The room as it always looked before Mrs. Clancy's arrival. ...

In that second I knew. Mrs. Clancy had not typed that message we had found. Mrs. Clancy had not been in our house today.

"What's wrong, girl?" George Mead demanded.

I jerked back to the window. Jeff still waited on Austin's bench, unsuspecting, waited there in the trap that had been set for him. I turned and ran from the room. Mead's voice thundered after me in the hall, bellowed as the elevator inched down the fifteen stories.

My heart pounding in my throat, I tore through the traffic on the Avenue, clambered over the park wall, stumbled down the slope that led to the lake ... the broad expanse of water that was between me and that bench on the hilltop.

The knoll was deserted except for Jeff. At the foot of it a nurse played with her small charge. A man held down a cloud of multi-colored balloons near by. Another man, sitting on the same bench where I had sat while Austin Marshall was being murdered, read a newspaper. But even from my distance I could recognize that figure. Its roly-poly plumpness was unmistakable. Bernard Marshall was sitting at the foot of the hill, motionless, waiting.

I was racing around the walk that skirted the lake, bumping into baby carriages and bicycles and children. I left the walk and ran on the grass beside it ... ran faster than I had ever run in my life.

Bernard Marshall had risen now; he tossed the newspaper on the bench behind him. If he started up the steps he would reach Jeff before I could. Jeff wouldn't see him; he had turned, his back was toward the lake. I tried to shout; my winded lungs couldn't raise a sound that topped the screams of the playing children.

Then I saw another figure and I almost collapsed with relief. A park attendant had turned off the walk, he was climbing the hillside. He moved slowly, spearing up fallen papers with his stick, but he would reach the top before Bernard. Jeff would be safe for a little while … for long enough.

The park man was at the top now. If he would stay there … if he would only stay. He was tall and straight, his back was broad. Jeff and he, the two of them, could handle the murderer whatever weapon he might use. The man half-turned, then moved again toward Jeff. He stretched out his stick to spear a piece of paper. The sunlight glinted off it and I screamed.

The thing he carried was not a length of broom handle with a nail in its end. It was smooth and highly polished; it was a malacca walking stick tipped with a murderous sliver of steel. It was Tony Gilbert moving toward Jeff, just as he had moved toward Austin Marshall.

My scream sent the stick up into the air, up above Jeff's back. Then Jeff was in motion. He threw his body sideways in a rolling, sprawling dive that hit Tony at the ankles and kicked his feet from under him. Instantly, Tony was up and running, running wildly down the steps toward me. He stumbled, tried desperately to right himself, then hurtled headfirst down upon the concrete walk. He lay there at my feet, his eyes closed. Jeff, the malacca stick in his hands, bent over his unconscious body.

CHAPTER SIXTEEN

IT WAS twenty minutes after nine by our kitchen clock when Jeff returned from Centre Street. There were no medals pinned on his chest, but I could tell from his face that Hankins had been saying some very nice things. A kind word from the taciturn detective, fortunately, meant more to Jeff than a thousand dollars. I placed a Tom Collins in my tired but triumphant husband's hand and a kiss on his forehead.

"I'm glad to see you," I said. "I'm glad you got Tony before he got you. I'm glad."

"Say, how'd you like that block I threw at him? You know, I think I'm a better athlete now than I was ..."

"Oh, dear," I sighed. "I can see you're going to be impossible to live with, simply impossible. I'll have to lower you a peg. You didn't know that Tony was the murderer until he tried to kill you, did you, dear? You didn't ..."

"I did know! I'm not only physical, I'm mental! I wish I could remember the FBI man's exact words ... anyway, he congratulated me, heartily."

"The FBI! How do they figure in this?"

"They arrested Walter Davisson. And his wife, Marjorie."

"But why? I don't ..."

"The Davissons were working for the enemy. And Tony Gilbert was working for the Davissons."

"The Marriage Doctor ... his charming Marjorie ... and Tony! They're Nazis? Is that what you are saying, Jeff?"

"Right. Then, Tony, of course, murdered Austin Marshall. In the line of duty. Tony admitted everything. What a performance! He seemed to almost enjoy his confession, played it straight to the gallery. It was kind of gruesome."

I took a long pull on my drink. "Jeff, you ... single-handed ... trapped three Nazi agents. Is that what I am to understand?"

"Well, the FBI had been suspicious of the Davissons for some time. And they knew it. That accounts for the Smuggler."

"Slower, Jeff. Haila isn't what she used to be."

"All right. Mrs. Davisson met Tony while sailing boats at the park. She sized him up for what he was ... a guy who would do anything for money. So Tony went to work. While entertaining at the canteens and the naval bases, the army camps and war plants, he picked up military information. For instance, when a convoy was leaving New York, where it was going, what it was carrying. He'd get the information to Davisson via his model ship and Marjorie. Then Davisson, as the Marriage Doctor, would radio the information in code to the Nazis. German U-boat commanders probably simply loved the Marriage Doctor's programs!"

I shook my head and took another drink.

Jeff said, "Since both Tony and Marjorie had been sailing model ships for years, it was a natural way for him to smuggle his information to her. And a safe way. He and Marjorie stayed apart, were never seen speaking to each other anyplace. The FBI was investigating everyone connected with the Davissons but they had no way of ever connecting Tony with them. And if their boat hanky-panky should ever be discovered, they would do exactly what they did to us. Pretend to be two clandestine lovers foiling a jealous husband."

"Jeff, when did you see through that?"

"This morning on the bus when we passed the lake. You said something about Tony and Marjorie's date on Thursday, remember?"

"Yes. The date he spoke of in the note we saw. They were to meet at nine-thirty at the Algonquin … Jeff! Tony couldn't have met her then! He would be at the theater, playing his show!"

"Sure. And Tony knew that. Therefore, that statement had to mean something else. What else could it be but a code? The reason the whole thing sounded more like a travelogue than a love letter was because it was a code. Code, Haila, think. Decoding … cryptography."

"Cryptography … Austin?"

"Yes. One of his hobbies was decoding, we knew that. Well, what if Mrs. Davisson had been lying, what if Austin *had* found a note in the Smuggler on Sunday? He'd know at once that there was something phony about it; he'd probably recognize it as a code right away. Suppose that note, decoded, would uncover something that Tony would murder to keep hidden? I was stuck there until I remembered that Austin had put on glasses when he sat down on the bench. He didn't wear them, Bernard said, except to read. But there wasn't anything to read near him when his body was found. That seemed to prove that whatever he had been reading was stolen from him. And then I was sure that Tony must have murdered him before he had a chance to decipher the note. But I still couldn't see how he did it without being noticed. And I didn't get that until I was on my way to the park this afternoon."

"How?" I asked. "Did you notice how much a park attendant's uniform looks like a soldier's fatigue outfit? Then remember Tony's costume in his play?"

"I did it like this. Why, when Tony had to murder Austin so quickly, did he take time to go to the theater first? What was there that he wanted … his makeup, his costume … then I had it. His uniform, without the blouse, would look like a park attendant's suit. His cane, fitted with a sharp nail, would be a pickup stick. It was like Tony with his supertheatricalism to commit his murder that way. He knew that no one pays any more attention to the park workmen than they do to the benches or trees; they're a part of the scenery. And he got an unexpected break when Phillips hid the true time of the crime for so long. By the time that came to light, no one could remember that a park attendant had climbed the hill.

"And that's how it was. On Sunday, Austin accidentally intercepted one of Tony's messages. And Austin, despite what Tony told us, cordially detested him for swindling him out of fifteen thousand dollars. Tony knew that Marshall would get to the bottom of that highly suspicious note business and do something about it. So he had to kill him fast … before he learned that Tony was working with the enemy.

"In his confession to Hankins, Tony said that he'd thought for a long time that posing as a park attendant would be the perfect way to commit a crime. And here was his chance to work it. He rushed to the theater, got into his costume, snitched a theater rubbish bag, surreptitiously used the stage carpenter's tools to fix his cane, and he was ready. On the street, he was a soldier. In the park, he unfolded his bag, adjusted his uniform and became a park employee. The nail stayed in Austin's neck when he was stabbed, but it was untraceable. Tony had still committed the perfect crime."

"You really thought it was perfect?"

"Sure I did. The break I got was seeing Mrs. Davisson remove the note from the Smuggler. Even then she fooled me. I believed her story. But she made a mistake showing me the note. Her husband realized that the moment he saw it. He decided that I had to be killed before I caught the flaw in it ... the Thursday night business. That's why he, posing as a distressed father, lured us over to Hoboken. Remember how explicit his directions to get to 479 Pine Street were? We were to pass a deserted building where two of his boys were waiting. We were to be disposed of promptly."

"That incompetent bus driver!" I said.

"Kiss him for me, Haila. If he hadn't taken us past our stop so that we approached 479 from another direction, well ... our bodies mightn't have been found for quite a while, if ever. Then we went back to the ferry in the ice, coal and wood truck, and Davisson's boys were completely frustrated. They reported their failure to Davisson. He threw caution to the winds and told Tony to put us out of the way, and quick, wherever and whenever he could. Tony went straight to work. He followed us to the park last night and nearly got me then."

"It wasn't Diane, then, who was ..."

"No. Her cute trick of trying to pin the murder on her husband didn't help solve this case any. But I'm grateful to her for one thing. It was her coming last night that interrupted Tony's plan to bump me off in my own home ... and you, too, if necessary. He followed us to the park; he shot and he missed. This afternoon he broke into our house to wait for us. Then Mrs. Clancy phoned to say she couldn't come today, and he took the message, pretending he was I. And that gave him his great idea. He would repeat his perfect crime. He left a fake message and hustled up to the theater to get ready for another murder performance."

"Jeff, did you know the message was a fake?"

"I had a hunch. And then, by the time I had figured out how Tony committed the crime, I was sure. I was waiting for him."

"And, Jeff, that scene Marjorie and Davisson pulled on us up at the radio station ... that was ..."

"That was brilliant ad libbing. Davisson never expected to see us again; Tony was to have knocked us off before that could happen. So when we popped up at the studio, he was trapped. But he got out of it with some wonderful collaboration from his wife. That domestic quarrel they had ... all the stuff about his fear that Marjorie's romance with Tony would ruin his radio program ...

his explanation for pulling the Nichols-Laura stunt ... all that was an act for our benefit."

"A benefit performance," I said. "And we loved it. And fell for it. But, darling, there's still one thing I don't understand. On Sunday night when our house was ransacked ... you hadn't even seen Tony's note then. It couldn't have been Tony in here."

"No, it wasn't Tony." Jeff got up and stretched.

"Who was it then? What was he after?"

"You know what he was after, my sweet. After the thousand dollars you picked out of my pocket."

"Oh, Jeff, you knew? You figured it out ..."

"Sure, I'm a detective."

"Well, then, suppose you figure out who stole it out of my tea canister! Jeff, you ... you ..."

One by one Jeff was dropping hundred dollar bills in my lap. "That was me on Sunday night. I stole it."

"But you chased someone out of the apartment!"

"I wanted to make sure you thought I did. I wanted to make sure you suffered, darling, for your wickedness. It's time you learned that crime does not pay!"

"I know it doesn't, dear ... seven hundred, eight hundred, nine hundred. ... Two of them must have stuck together. ... One hundred, two hundred ..."

THE END

If you enjoyed *Sailor, Take Warning!* the first three Jeff and Haila Troy mysteries by Kelley Roos may be purchased from the same bookseller who sold you this title: *Made Up To Kill* (0-915230-79-8, $14.95)
If the Shroud Fits (0-915230-92-5, $14.95), and
The Frightened Stiff (0-91523075-5, $14.95).
For more information on The Rue Morgue Press
please turn the page.

About the Rue Morgue Press

"Rue Morgue Press is the old-mystery lover's best friend, reprinting high quality books from the 1930s and '40s."
—*Ellery Queen's Mystery Magazine*

Since 1997, the Rue Morgue Press has reprinted scores of traditional mysteries, the kind of books that were the hallmark of the Golden Age of detective fiction. Authors reprinted or to be reprinted by the Rue Morgue include Dorothy Bowers, Pamela Branch, Joanna Cannan, Glyn Carr, Torrey Chanslor, Clyde B. Clason, Joan Coggin, Manning Coles, Lucy Cores, Frances Crane, Norbert Davis, Elizabeth Dean, Constance & Gwenyth Little, Marlys Millhiser, James Norman, Stuart Palmer, Craig Rice, Kelley Roos, Charlotte Murray Russell, Maureen Sarsfield, Margaret Scherf and Juanita Sheridan.

To suggest titles or to receive a catalog of Rue Morgue Press books write P.O. Box 4119, Boulder, CO 80306, telephone 800-699-6214, or check out our website, www.ruemorguepress.com, which lists complete descriptions of all of our titles, along with lengthy biographies of our writers.